ETERNITY'S WHEEL

ETERNITY'S

WHEEL

AN *INTERWORLD* NOVEL

story by

NEIL GAIMAN,
MICHAEL REAVES, AND
MALLORY REAVES

WRITTEN BY MICHAEL REAVES AND MALLORY REAVES

HarperCollins *Children's Books*

First published in the USA by HarperCollins Publishers Inc in 2015

First published in Great Britain by HarperCollins Children's Books in 2015

HarperCollins Children's Books is a division of HarperCollinsPublishers Ltd,

HarperCollins Publishers

1 London Bridge Street

London SE1 9GF

The HarperCollins Children's Books website address is

www.harpercollins.co.uk

1

HB ISBN 978-0-00-758195-5

TPB ISBN 978-0-00-752350-4

Printed and bound in England by

Clays Ltd, St Ives plc

For CAL COTTON
and THERESA MACWILLIE,
who I think must have had the ability to Walk between
conventions.
—Mallory Reaves

INTERLOG

Mom, Dad, Jenny, and Kevin the Squid,

I'm sorry.

I'm sorry I left and I'm sorry I can't come back, and for everything I'm sure you've been through in the past however many years. I'm sorry you were given this note and know I was here but left without saying hello or good-bye. I was never even supposed to come back—it was a fluke, a one-time thing, and the longer I stay, the more likely it is I'd put you in danger.

I shouldn't even be writing this. But I couldn't come back, even accidentally, and leave without saying I miss you. I think of you guys every day. I bet the Squid is so big now! You probably don't call him that anymore. If you do, when he's old enough, tell him I'm sorry he got stuck with the nickname. He can blame his older brother, even though he won't remember me.

Jenny, I hope you're enjoying my music collection, and everything else, really. I'm not coming back again, so everything is yours. I miss you, kid.

Dad, I'm sorry I didn't say good-bye when I left. It was hard enough to tell Mom, and I knew you wouldn't let me go. Everything I'm doing is to keep you all safe, even though you may not understand it. I'm doing it to keep everyone safe. I think you'd be proud of me.

Mom, I still have the necklace you gave me. It helps to remind me of home and what I'm fighting for. I met a girl. Her name is Acacia. I don't know if it's even . . . anything, but I think you'd like her. She's tough. She doesn't take crap from anybody, especially me.

I miss you all so much. I know the chances are astronomically slim, but I hope I can see you again someday. That thought is part of what keeps me going.

I love you.

J. H.

CHAPTER ONE

HAVE YOU EVER HAD to walk with a broken rib? If not, count yourself lucky—and if you have, I sympathize. If you've ever had to walk three blocks with a broken rib, wrist, and fractured shoulder, all while trying to make it look like you were out for a stroll in the park . . . well, then you and I should exchange stories sometime. For now, here's mine.

My name is Joseph Harker. I'm almost seventeen, and I'm back on my version of Earth for the first time in two years, if not longer. It's hard to tell exactly how much time has passed when you're hopping from world to world.

When I left, I gave up everything I'd ever known. My friends, my family, including the little brother who hadn't quite learned to say my name right yet. The possibility of straight As on my next report card. My favorite breakfast cereal and riding my bike through the crisp fall leaves on Saturday afternoons. My mother's smile, my father's laugh.

Everything I thought my life would be. Still, I gave it all up, and willingly.

I'd lost so much more than that in the past two days.

It was dark; the sun had just been going down when I'd arrived. I'd stayed in the park to watch the red-gold light set the familiar town afire one last time, then started off toward my school. My old school, I should say. "School" now was the long, sterile halls and compact rooms of InterWorld Base Town; the Hazard Zone combat sessions; and the trips that were all for field training. At least, it had been. Maybe Inter-World Base Town was my old school now, too.

No, I thought fiercely, as I concentrated on keeping my feet moving across the grass. I would get back there. I would see InterWorld again.

I had to.

Through the park, off the grass, onto the sidewalk. Even after being away for so long, I knew where I was going—which wasn't due to any innate sense of direction, believe me. I just knew that the park was between my house and my school, and I had landed house side instead of school side. Not too difficult, even for someone who might or might not have a concussion. I hadn't hit the ground from that far up when I'd been shoved through dimensions, but it'd sure *felt* like I had.

I kept moving, resisting the urge to keep my head down; the last thing I wanted to do was draw attention to myself. I didn't know how my parents had explained my absence these last two years, but I couldn't risk being recognized. I was here to see one person, and one person only. Someone who had helped me through any number of crazy situations even *before* I had turned into an interdimensional freedom fighter.

My social studies teacher.

His house was right next to the school, and I only knew where *that* was because he'd made it a point to tell every kid in his class that if they ever needed anything, day or night, his address was 1234, the same street the school was on. I once asked if he'd picked that number on purpose so it would be easy for us to remember. He shook his head and said, "No, I picked it on purpose so it would be easy for *me* to remember."

1218 . . . 1220 . . . It was getting harder and harder to move without stumbling, but I did my best. There were still a few people out walking dogs or supervising young children. I could see a familiar-looking green Jeep in the distance, parked at the end of a short driveway. 1226 . . . 1230 . . . Almost there. I reached the mailbox marked 1234, stepped around the Jeep, and went up to the front door. The lights were out.

Please be home, I thought, pressing the doorbell. After a moment I pressed it again, and then I sagged against the wall. He was probably still at the school, grading papers. I should have gone there first. I wasn't sure I could make it there now.

I stood there for a few minutes, weighing my options. Could I wait? *Should* I wait?

"Joey?"

My knees almost buckled, though it was with relief rather than fatigue. I knew that voice.

I lifted my head, turning to see my former social studies teacher, Mr. Dimas, standing there holding a laptop bag in one hand and a stack of papers in another. "Joseph Harker?" he asked again, and I nodded.

"Mr. Dimas," I said. "I need help."

He peered at me over the rim of his glasses, apparently trying to figure out if I was on the level. I must have looked pitiful, or at least harmless, because he nodded and moved past me to unlock the door without another word. He didn't seem any older . . . but then, last time I'd been at InterWorld for about five months, I'd only been gone from *here* for two days. I wasn't sure how the time discrepancy would translate from two *years*, but I didn't feel like doing the math. Come to think of it, for all I knew I could have been thrown back (or even forward) in time; I hadn't come here on purpose, after all. Could they even do that?

That was an unsettling thought. I was used to not knowing *where* I was, but I'd never really had to question *when* I was. Not until my recent association with a Time Agent, anyway.

Acacia. God, I was worried about her.

Mr. Dimas led me inside, turning on the hall light and gesturing for me to sit on his couch. I started to, but hesitated. I could feel the sticky, warm, wet feeling of blood matting the back of my shirt under my hoodie. "I might get blood on it," I said, and he fixed me with a long look. I could tell what he was probably thinking: that I wasn't *visibly* bleeding (except for the cuts on my wrist, which I'd kept in my pocket on the way over), but if I was worried about staining his couch it might be worse than it looked.

"It's just a deep scratch, I think," I said. He sighed.

"Ordinarily I wouldn't care about furniture stains, but they still haven't closed the case on your disappearance. One moment—take off your sweatshirt, if you can." He left the room.

I stayed where I was, dizzy from all the sudden implications. Of course my disappearance would have been reported to the police; I'd been young enough when I'd left to still be considered truant. I'd told Mom and Mr. Dimas the truth, and Mom would have told Dad and maybe Jenny, but there's no way they would have been able to tell anyone else.

"No one's being blamed for it, are they?" I blurted out as Mr. Dimas came back into the room. He was carrying two trash bags and a roll of duct tape.

"No," he said immediately, and I relaxed a hair as he started to tape the trash bags over his couch. "Your parents reported you as a runaway two days after you left, but the police still looked into everyone you had contact with. Someone saw you come in to talk to me after school the night you disappeared, so they've investigated me more thoroughly."

"I'm sorry," I said, unable to think of anything else to say.

"No need to apologize. Your mother has firmly and publicly stated she does not believe I had any involvement in your disappearance, which has helped. It isn't as though they suspect me of murder or anything, though they *will* if you get your blood on my furniture." He finished the last of the taping and stepped back, nodding to himself. "Sit," he told me, and I did. The plastic crinkled beneath me, but all the cloth was covered. I leaned back, with no small amount of relief. My ribs were killing me.

He sat down across from me in a comfortable-looking armchair, and leaned forward to assist me in removing my sweatshirt, like he'd told me to do before. "I don't know where to start," he said. I wasn't sure if he was talking about my injuries, or my story.

"Neither do I," I admitted.

"Why did you come to me, instead of your family?"

"I can't stay," I said immediately. The answer was that simple, really. I couldn't stay, and my family would want me to. *I'd* want me to. It wouldn't be fair to raise their expectations, give them false hope that I was back for good, or that I could at least visit for a while. I wasn't, and I couldn't, for their own safety.

He was nodding, accepting my answer and the unspoken reasons behind it. "Okay. That scrape doesn't look too bad;

you're not going to bleed out if I run to the drugstore. What do you need?"

"Ah." I hesitated, trying to think. "My right wrist is definitely broken, and some of my ribs might be. I also might have a concussion; I fell pretty hard a few . . . on the way over here," I stumbled, not wanting to give him the impression I'd been in trouble right before coming to his door. "My shoulder was fractured"—I paused, trying to figure out how long ago it had been—"in a rockslide," I said, stalling. "It was tended to and mostly healed, but it's still aching."

"How long ago was it seen to?"

It was so hard to tell. The last few days were a blur of places and people and injuries, and I hadn't slept or eaten with any kind of regularity. "Ah . . . a week ago? Two? I'm not sure," I admitted.

"I'll get you some aspirin. A brace for your wrist is the best I can do, since I'm assuming you don't want me to take you to the hospital." I shook my head, and he continued. "I'll get medical tape for your ribs, but if one of them *is* broken, the best you can do is not move for a while." He eyed me. "I take it that's not an option?"

I shook my head again.

"I'm leaving as soon as I can stand again," I said.

"To where?"

"Another dimension," I said. "Somewhere I might be able

to find help." I'd already told him some of it, after all.

"I see," he said, and stood up. He sounded regretful, and offered his hand. I took it with my left one, not really sure why. "Joseph Harker," he said, "I've never been sure if you're crazy or if I am, but I'm glad to know you either way."

"Thank you, sir," I said, and he paused at the honorific. It was habit for me; I'd gotten used to calling the Old Man that. To his face, anyway. "Mr. Dimas," I amended.

"Call me Jack," he said. "I'm not your teacher anymore."

I wasn't sure what to say, so I nodded. He patted his jacket to make sure he had his wallet, and moved toward the door. "If you can wait on the aspirin, I'll pick up some extra-strength painkillers."

"That'd be great," I said, though the thought of waiting a few more minutes wasn't awesome. Still, I'd live, and it would be better for me in the long run.

"I'll be back," he said. I nodded again, even though he wasn't looking at me anymore, and listened as the front door opened and closed behind him. I heard the click of his key in the lock. I wasn't sure if he was locking me in or making sure to keep everyone else out. Probably both.

I'll admit it: I was nervous about going to *anyone* for help. Not only was it entirely possible he'd be coming back with some nice men in pristine white coats but there was no telling what kind of trouble I might have brought with me. My enemies had sent me here on purpose, which meant they probably wouldn't be coming after me . . . *probably*. There was no way to know for sure. Even aside from that, I had already had one teammate turn on me in recent memory. I was having a few trust issues right now, not that I think anyone would blame me.

I tilted my head back against the covered couch, listening to the crinkle of plastic around my ears. I was dizzy. What I really needed was to sleep for about a decade, but I'd probably get about an hour. I'd been sent here to witness the destruction of everything. I didn't know how soon they were planning on making that happen, but I probably couldn't afford to rest for too long.

Despite that thought, I must have passed out on the couch while I was waiting for Mr. Dimas—Jack—to get back from the store. One moment I was sitting there, thinking about how I couldn't rest for long, and the next I was hearing the key in the lock again and realizing I'd fallen asleep.

And I woke up with a headache, which is pretty much the worst thing *ever*.

"How long were you gone?" I asked, as he stepped into my line of sight.

He looked at his watch. "Twenty-three minutes," he said, raising an eyebrow at me. "Are you okay?"

"Water and painkillers," I said. "Please."

He brought me a bottle of water and two maximum-strength aspirins. I swallowed them both at once, along with half the water. Mr. Dimas (I kept thinking of him that way, no matter what he'd said) was laying out supplies on the table: a wrist brace, an Ace bandage, medical tape, butterfly bandages, gauze, disinfectant, etc.

"Tell me what happened," he said, sitting on the table across from me and dabbing the disinfectant on the gauze.

"It's not going to make much sense to you," I said apologetically.

"That's fine. Just talk to me. This is going to hurt."

Oh. I nodded, trying to figure out where to start. I had told him some the last time I'd been home, before I'd made the decision to fully commit my life to InterWorld. . . . "How much do you remember from what I told you before?"

"I've never forgotten it," he said. "You went missing for a day and a half, and then you came to see me at school one evening with a story about how you'd discovered you could travel through dimensions."

"We call it Walking," I said. He was cleaning the cuts on my wrist left by Lord Dogknife's claws, and they were starting to sting. A lot.

"Right. You were being chased by this magic organization. . . ."

"HEX," I filled in. "They're the bad guys. One of them, anyway."

"And you were rescued by an older version of you, who was killed in the process."

"Jay," I said, the ache of the words and the memories nothing compared to the stinging of my wounds. Thinking of Jay no longer hurt as much as it used to; everything healed eventually. "And I brought his body back to InterWorld. That's where I met the other versions of me."

"Because you all have the same power," he said.

"Right. See, since *I* have the power to Walk between dimensions, every other version of me in every other dimension has that same power. I don't know why me—or, why *us*—but there it is. We can all do it, some better than others. Apparently, I'm . . . pretty good at it."

"Which is how you did it by accident at first," he said, pinching my skin together as he placed a butterfly bandage over the worst of the cuts. I continued to speak, watching him with a vague, detached fascination. "And then you went on a training mission, correct? The one that turned out to be a trap?"

"Yeah. Everyone got captured by HEX, except for me. I only escaped because of Hue."

"Your little extraterrestrial friend. You called him an . . . MDLF?"

"Yeah, M-D-L-F, standing for multidimensional life-form, or mudluff. He's not an extraterrestrial, exactly, he's a . . . well, a multidimensional life-form. He looks kind of like a big soap bubble, and communicates by changing colors, so I call him Hue. Or her, I really don't know. . . ." I stopped talking for a moment, taking slow, even breaths. Mr. Dimas was cleaning the scrape along my side. I didn't even remember getting that one, but it was hurting quite a bit now that he'd found it. Fights were like that; half the time you didn't feel your bruises until later.

"Your team was captured by HEX," he prompted me, and I closed my eyes to concentrate.

"Yeah. Except for me, because of Hue. But it still seemed pretty suspicious, so the Old Man—he's our leader, another version of me—wiped my memories and sent me back here. That's when I showed up again after almost two days and came to talk to you."

"Because you'd gotten your memories back."

"Yeah. Hue came and found me, and seeing him, I just . . . remembered everything. I guess they couldn't take that away from me, for some reason. . . ."

"So this mudluff creature came here," Mr. Dimas said, looking interested, "to our Earth."

"Yeah. I don't know if they do that all the time, or if it was because I was here, or . . ."

"Where is Hue now?"

"I don't know. He's kind of like a stray cat. He hangs around when he wants attention or if I'm upset and he's trying to help, and he's saved my life more than once, but sometimes he disappears for days or weeks at a time."

Mr. Dimas nodded, gesturing for me to sit up. I did so,

gingerly, and he started to rub some sort of minty-smelling gel onto my ribs. "For the bruising," he explained. "Tell me what happened after you went back to InterWorld."

"Well, I thought I'd remembered everything at first, but I couldn't *quite* grasp the way back to Base Town. So instead I tracked down where the rest of my team had been taken, and we all managed to escape." It was an incredibly condensed, watered-down version of what had actually happened, but it was true enough. I had tracked my team through the Nowhere-at-All to a nightmarish HEX battleship, gotten myself recaptured, caused a ruckus in the prison cells, set hundreds of captive souls free, and more or less accidentally destroyed the entire ship. There had been some quick thinking and a few almost heroic moments, but most of it had been dumb luck.

"Go on," Mr. Dimas urged. He was wrapping the tape around my ribs now, which hurt nine ways from Sunday.

"Uh, so, we escaped . . . and I was accepted back into InterWorld. It's been about two years for me. I've been training, going on various missions, doing okay in my studies . . . business as usual. Nothing too weird happened until my team and I were sent to retrieve some data from a Binary world last . . . ugh, I don't even know. A week ago? Two, maybe?" It was so hard to keep track. . . .

"Binary world?"

"Binary are like HEX: bad guys. They're two different

factions who both want the same thing, though the Binary are what they sound like: machines, mostly, run by a sentient computer who calls itself zero-one-one-zero-one, or 'the Professor.' They're the science; HEX is the magic."

He glanced up at me over his glasses. "Magic?"

I couldn't help giving a small grin. "Yeah. I had the same reaction, but I've seen it. Magic. I could go into how it works and what it is and all that, but it doesn't really matter. It *works* and it *is*, and HEX has the monopoly on it—except for the fringe worlds closer to the high end of the Arc, but—"

"You're losing me," he said, tying off the end of the tape now wrapped firmly around my torso.

"I'm losing myself, I think," I said, trying to concentrate on breathing. I was starting to get tunnel vision.

"Sit back for a minute," he advised, looking me over. "And drink more water."

I nodded, following his advice. At least the pills were kicking in, and I could feel my headache starting to ebb. They weren't doing too much for the rest of me, though.

"What's this?" he asked suddenly. I turned my head; he'd found the small bruise and little puncture wound of an injection site on my arm.

"Ah, that. I got injected with a tracer for safety reasons, after the rockslide. It's advanced technology, it'll dissolve harmlessly within another week or so."

"Nothing that needs my attention?" I shook my head.

"All right. What's a fringe world?" he asked, once I started to feel less like I was going to pass out.

"It's . . . it was explained to me like this: the Multiverse is *everything*. Think of it kind of like the moon: a giant circle, partly in shadow. The shadowed part is the Altiverse. The bright part, like a crescent moon, is the Arc. The Arc has all the main versions of our universe, with our Earth, and they vary from high magic to high science, depending on where they are in the Arc. That's mostly because HEX and Binary each rule over opposite sides, but they're trying to rule over ALL of it. We call those worlds, closer to one side or the other, fringe worlds. Make sense?"

He was nodding, though he looked a bit dazed. I suppose I couldn't blame him; I'd essentially just given him hard facts about our much-speculated cosmology. I'd probably rocked his world a bit. "Go on," he said.

"Okay. Um . . ." I paused. I'd been explaining about fringe worlds, but why . . . ? "Right, magic versus science, or HEX versus Binary. The Professor is the leader of the Binary; HEX's leader is a . . . kind of like a demonic dog. They call him Lord Dogknife. He's the one who did most of this damage." I held up my wrist and indicated my ribs. "And sent me back here."

"Okay. So, you said you were sent to retrieve some data from a Binary world?" He started to wrap the Ace bandage around my wrist.

"Right, yes. We weren't able to get the data; there were too many rutabagas—that's what we call Binary soldiers; they're basically unintelligent clones—and it was looking like things were about to get bad. Then this girl appeared. Dark hair, violet eyes. I'd never seen her before, but she rescued us. Her name was—is—Acacia Jones. She's a . . . an agent for another organization." It occurred to me, sort of all at once, that perhaps telling him about TimeWatch wasn't the best idea. I knew next to nothing about it, aside from the fact that it was called TimeWatch, they'd once sent me thousands of years into the future, and Acacia was something called a Time Agent. It seemed like the sort of thing that might be pretty classified.

Mr. Dimas looked like he might be about to ask a question, but I kept talking. "I showed her around InterWorld a bit, but then I had to go out on another mission. Another Walker—that's what I am, a Walker—was found on the same Binary world we'd just been trying to get the information from. The Old Man sent us back to get the info and the Walker." I remembered all of that quite vividly. Crawling through the air vents in the shut-down office building, finding the other version of me held captive, feeling an instant connection . . . "His name was Joaquim," I said, feeling my stomach churn. There was a sour taste in my mouth, though whether from the remembered betrayal or the lingering pain of my injuries, I couldn't be sure. I sat still for a moment, just breathing. Just remembering.

"Joseph?" Mr. Dimas asked, pausing as he reached over to pick up the wrist brace.

"I'm fine," I lied, taking another drink of water. "Long story short, we thought Joaquim was one of us, but he wasn't. He was a clone, like the rutabagas Binary makes, but infused with souls and powered by HEX's magic. That was when we discovered HEX and Binary were working together." I shook my head, the weight of it all descending upon me once again. The only thing that had given InterWorld a fighting chance was HEX and Binary's war with each other. Now that they'd called a truce, however temporary it might be, they'd be turning all their focus on us.

"Infused with souls?" Mr. Dimas repeated, looking at me seriously.

"Yeah," I said bleakly. "HEX and Binary keep the souls of any Walker they catch. Apparently, that's the source of our power, the very essence of what we are. They use us to power their ships, so they can travel between dimensions as well."

"So they made a clone of you."

"Using Jay's blood from where he'd died."

"And powered him with . . ."

"The souls of dead Walkers."

"Okay," he said, looking grim. He shook his head. "So he wasn't really one of you."

"No. He was sabotaging InterWorld from within. He

caused a rockslide during a training mission that injured a bunch of us"—I gestured to my shoulder—"and killed a friend of mine. His name was Jerzy."

"I'm sorry," said Mr. Dimas. I nodded.

"HEX and Binary were using Joaquim to try and power a . . . HEX called it FrostNight. It . . . was basically created to restart the universe. So they could make it into whatever they wanted."

Mr. Dimas looked like he was having trouble grasping this. I didn't blame him. "Restart the *universe*?"

"Or the Multiverse, depending on how far they got. I . . . Acacia and I tried to stop it, but . . ."

"Did you?"

"I—I can't assume we did."

"I imagine we'd know if you hadn't. Or, perhaps we wouldn't know, but we also wouldn't be here?"

"Maybe. I don't know how fast it moves, or . . . It's a soliton, which means it will maintain a continuous speed without losing momentum or energy . . . or, that's what they told me. So it would still take a while to erase *everything*."

"I see. How did you try to stop it, or is that too complicated?"

"They were trying to use Joaquim *and me*," I admitted, holding up my other hand. The skin around my wrist was still chafed raw from where I'd gotten out of the restraints. "I got out, with Acacia's help," I added quickly, seeing he was about to ask. I didn't want to tell him the truth: that while Acacia *had* helped me, it hadn't been her who'd broken the machine. It had been me. Thousands of me, scattered through the air like fireflies . . .

I'd used the souls. I'd called them to me, added their power to mine, and directed them to do as I wished. I still wasn't sure if the ends had justified the means, or if it made me just like the monsters I fought against.

"So you think, without you, it may not have been powered completely?"

"Maybe, but like I said, I can't assume that."

Mr. Dimas nodded again. "What happened after you got out?"

"We tried to go back to InterWorld, but we couldn't get there. The Old Man had figured out Joaquim's energy drain on the ship, and thrown the engines into overdrive to get away. We were waiting for our ship to pick us up when we saw it warp away, followed by a HEX ship. It's . . . that HEX found InterWorld Base Town is . . ."

"Bad, I imagine?"

"Very bad." I watched as he secured the wrist brace around my hand. It hurt, but I relaxed immediately now that I didn't have to concentrate on trying not to move it too much. "Inter-World might be able to stay ahead of the HEX ship, but they're gonna have to keep running, which means they're essentially trapped. They can't stop, not even for a second."

"Let me see if I have anything for that burn on your wrist and the one on your side." Mr. Dimas stood, leaving me in momentary confusion. What burn on my side? I shifted, finding the rough texture along my skin, and the pain that came with it. *Right* . . . It was from J/O's laser. That was something I'd left out of the retelling. My teammate J/O, a cyborg version of me, had been turned against us by a Binary virus. Acacia had saved me from him, too, left him wandering through time looking for us. . . .

"He wasn't on the ship," I said suddenly, as Mr. Dimas sat back down across from me.

"Who wasn't?"

"J/O. A teammate of mine, he's a cyborg me," I explained, only half listening to what I was saying. My brain was moving too fast for my mouth. "He'd been infected by a Binary virus and was working with Joaquim. He attacked me—that's where I got the burn on my side from his laser cannon—but Acacia threw us through time and he couldn't find us . . . but that means he wasn't on Base Town when they had to punch it, he must have been left behind. He's still out there somewhere—" I stopped, not wanting to alarm him, but the sentence continued on in my head. *He could come find me. He could come* here.

"I have to go," I said, but Mr. Dimas was shaking his head.

"Not with your injuries," he said firmly, putting a hand on my fractured shoulder when I tried to stand up. I winced, and he gave me a look that said *see?* "You can barely walk, and what little medical attention I've given you won't help much unless you *sleep and heal*."

"You might be in danger," I tried.

"You *are* in danger, and you're not going to get out of it without dying unless you rest, not to mention eat." He fixed me with a stern look over the top of his glasses, the look I remembered from sitting in his classroom.

My stomach gave a loud growl just then, as if to punctuate his sentence. I glanced down, betrayed, and felt heat rise to my face. "Okay," I said quietly, making the decision to leave as soon as I'd eaten. I wasn't going to put him in more danger than I already had, and besides, I had things to do. My army wasn't going to gather itself.

"Good," he said, straightening up. "Now. Important question: What do you want to eat?"

"I—" I stopped, it suddenly occurring to me that I could have anything I wanted. InterWorld kept us fed, of course; protein bars and enhanced vitamin water, very nutritious and not at all delicious. But I was *home* now, back on my world, and I could have anything. "Pizza," I said. I know it's cliché, but cut me some slack—I'm a teenage boy. What would *you* have asked for? Broccoli?

"I'm not surprised. What do you want on it?"

"Pepperoni and broccoli," I said. Shut up, it actually sounded good.

Mr. Dimas left to get the pizza ("I'll go pick it up," he'd said, "and you'd better be here when I get back, Joseph. I mean it.") and I relaxed back on the couch again, seriously considering passing out. Instead I forced my mind into some semblance of meditation. It was the best I could do right then; I was still exhausted and hurting and worried, and every passing car or creak of the house settling made me jump.

Even with all my injuries and fears and concerns, I couldn't stop thinking about Acacia. I hadn't gotten to that part of the story in my retelling to Mr. Dimas, of how we'd been standing together watching the HEX ship stalk its InterWorld prey, and Lord Dogknife had attacked from out of nowhere. . . . She hadn't even seen him coming. I didn't know what he'd done to her, except that the second time he'd knocked her down, his claws were slick with blood and she hadn't gotten back up.

I remembered her expression just before we'd been attacked. Most of my memories of her were like that, actually, moments of action frozen in time. I remembered her grinning at me a second before the sound of laser fire filled the air when J/O had found us; I remembered the way her face had been tilted toward mine before Lord Dogknife had attacked. I leaned back against the couch, remembering how she and I had sat back-to-back in a moment of respite, both of us injured, talking strategy and keeping each other going. I wondered if our friendship (relationship?) would be any different if we hadn't formed the majority of it while running for our lives.

Most of all, I wondered where she was now. I didn't know if she'd vanished of her own volition or if Lord Dogknife had sent her away or if she'd been rescued. I didn't know what the chances of seeing her again were, and I wondered if I ever would at all.

The rest of the night went by in a daze. I ate five slices of pizza and downed three bottles of water, as well as two more painkillers. Mr. Dimas had tended my injuries, fed me, and let me use his shower. He gave me his guest room (after making sure I wasn't going to bleed on anything) and made me promise not to leave without telling him. I finally collapsed into bed around nine, still dizzy from the whirlwind of events.

I remember that the food tasted good, and I remember enjoying it, but I was hard-pressed to remember what it had actually tasted *like*. My body was working overtime trying to heal, and in order to do that, it had to make me sleep.

I was afraid to. I'm not gonna lie, I've seen things that would give the devil himself nightmares (if he even existed anywhere; that kind of theology was something we'd never really gotten into in basic studies), and I'd come through the other side just fine. Now, though . . . not only was I afraid of the dreams I might have, I was afraid of something coming to find me. I was afraid of being so exhausted that I'd sleep right through something breaking in and hurting Mr. Dimas before it ever even got to me.

That, ultimately, was why I was here instead of with my family. Because I couldn't risk danger coming right to their door, to Mom and Dad and my little siblings. But my social studies teacher? Apparently I was willing to risk him.

Utterly disgusted with myself, I fell into an uneasy sleep.

CHAPTER TWO

I MUST HAVE SLEPT deeply for at least a few hours, because the first time I startled awake at a noise was around three A.M.

It had been a quiet noise, the kind you can't really identify once you're awake even though you know it's what woke you up. It might have been a thump or a creak. . . . Had I shut the door when I went to sleep, or left it ajar? It was open now.

The bed jiggled as something jumped up onto it, and I bolted upright, simultaneously aggravating my injuries and startling the hell out of a cat.

"Right, cat . . . Mr. Dimas has a cat," I mumbled, staring at the creature hunched down near my feet. It was an orange tabby whose name I didn't remember, but I recalled him using the cat's habit of bringing in dead mice and birds as a parallel lesson for something or other in his class.

I took a deep breath and looked out the window. No sign

of sunlight anywhere. I pushed myself out of bed, testing my balance and the general functionality of all my limbs. I was incredibly sore, but I could move. I'd had a plan before I even got to Mr. Dimas's, and now that I was in slightly better shape, I could get started. It was time to go collect my first recruit.

I know I'd promised, but I really didn't have a choice. Mr. Dimas would try to convince me to stay, and it was better for everyone if I didn't.

Still, there was something I had to do before I left.

Since I was staying in a teacher's house, it wasn't hard to find paper and a pencil. The cat followed me around as I put my socks and shoes back on, and he purred and nuzzled against my hand as I tried to gather my things. I couldn't help but smile. I'd always liked animals, and the cat reminded me of Hue. Sometimes when the mudluff wanted attention, he'd just get in the way of whatever I was doing.

I had two letters to write. The most important one was also the hardest, so I put it off until last. Instead, leaning against a desk with the cat winding itself around my ankles, I wrote:

> *Mr. Dimas (Jack),*
> *Sorry to run out like this, but you had to have expected I would. I know I promised, but it's safer for you and my family if I'm not on this world anymore.*

Speaking of my family, the other letter here is for them. Please make sure they get it.

Thank you for everything you've done for me, first and foremost not assuming I was crazy when I brought you this whole harebrained tale. The supplies will help immensely, and I'm sure I won't be the only one who'll be grateful for them.

Not much else to say. I know it sounds (again) crazy, but if the world is ever destroyed, you'll know I've failed in my mission. I'll do the best I can to make sure I don't.

Thanks again.

I debated signing my name for a few moments—it could be seen as incriminating, but Mr. Dimas was smart enough to burn the letter after he'd read it. Still, I decided not to chance it. He'd know who it was from.

I made my way silently out to the living room, grabbing the rust-red backpack he'd filled with granola bars, bottled water, and medical supplies for me. Another thing I was grateful for, particularly the aspirin. I stopped long enough to take two of those, then slipped soundlessly out through one of the windows so I wouldn't leave his front door unlocked. It seemed the least I could do.

The cat sat on the windowsill, watching as I made my way alone down the dark street.

The park was the best place to Walk from. It had a lot of wide-open space but enough trees that I could easily slip into a ring of them and not get caught disappearing—or reappearing, as the case may be. Many of my InterWorld lessons had explained that I had an instinctive navigational system for Walking, sort of like when you close your eyes and can still tell you're about to run into a wall. The chance of trying to Walk between dimensions and ending up occupying the same space as a car or trash can—or another person—was slim to none, but Walking in a wide-open space made it far *less* likely.

There was no moon tonight, though there were a few scattered streetlights. It was light enough to see, but dark enough that someone would have to get fairly close to recognize me. Unfortunately, since Greenville is a small town, any local police officers passing by might decide to stop and ask what I was doing out here at this time of night. I avoided the few cars on the road just in case. Finally, I stood in the park, breathing deeply. I wanted to smell what my old life had been like one last time.

Greenville is close to a huge river, and there was always mist in the early morning, even during the summer. It always smelled like wet grass and damp asphalt at night. There was the faintest hint of gasoline from the station down the street and the warm, sweet smell of the doughnut shop in the opposite direction. The shop opened at five A.M., so the owner, Mr. Lee, started baking at around three. The doughnuts were almost always gone by seven thirty, but if you stopped by on the way to school and he had one left, he'd give it to you for free.

I breathed carefully in and carefully out, committing everything to memory once again. Then I Walked, whispering a quiet good-bye to that sleepy little town.

Walking between dimensions, once you get used to it, is like walking normally—except easier, if that makes sense. Better. It feels *right*, like a good, satisfying stretch. It feels like doing what you were born to do.

I felt cold mist on my skin and heard a few tinkling notes, like from a music box. Random sensations are common when Walking, since you have to pass through the In-Between in order to get anywhere, and the In-Between is . . . well, it's pretty much everything. At once. It's the place we pass through when we Walk, sort of like its own pocket dimension. Or, more accurately, the dimension between all dimensions.

The park was spread out before me, looking almost the same as it had a moment ago. There was a tree about a hundred yards in front of me that hadn't been there before, but that was the only notable difference, at least at first. I started moving through the park, glancing around with fascination as the tiny changes became more noticeable.

I didn't smell the doughnut shop anymore; instead, the scent of freshly brewed coffee wafted over me from a twenty-four-hour diner across the street. I had to admit I was jealous. *My* Greenville didn't have a twenty-four-hour anything.

I walked to the corner, crossing the street at the protected crosswalk. The little light-up man was blue, not white as I was used to. I'd missed that the last time I'd been here. I passed by a McDonald's with arches that were green instead of yellow. I had to smile; that was the first thing I'd noticed when I first wound up in this version of my town.

I hurried as I went down my street. My injuries weren't bothering me as much as they had been (aspirin for the win!), and I needed to get this done as quickly as possible. The first time I'd come here, I'd run into the first other version of me I'd ever met. A girl. Josephine.

I remembered her name like I remembered my own, because in a way, it sort of was. I'd gone into my house, lost and confused, and there she'd been. She'd lived in my house with my mom, who'd looked at me like she'd never seen me before and called her daughter Josephine. Her daughter, not her son. A female version of me, living a life parallel to mine.

She would be my first recruit.

I was about halfway to my house when I stopped to cast out for her. We can sense each other, sort of, like when you're alone in a room but you can tell when someone walks in without turning around. I paused for a second and closed my eyes, expanding my senses, and that's probably what saved my life.

They'd been waiting for me.

I threw myself to the side as a netlike thing hurtled over where I'd been standing. They started to come up out of the shadows, or maybe they were the shadows themselves. It was hard to tell. All I knew for sure was that they were agents of HEX, and they had found me.

There were maybe four or five of them. I was trained in thirteen different styles of martial arts and immediately recognized six nearby objects that could be used as improvised weapons.

I also had no defensive gadgets on me whatsoever, and I was injured in five different places. Not to mention these were HEX agents, not Binary. The Binary at least were predictable; they had their plasma guns, their sheer numbers and one-shot shields, their grav disks. Basic stuff. HEX agents? Those were unpredictable. I'd taken three different Magic Study courses on InterWorld Prime, and I probably knew about a quarter of what they could do.

I was more than a little outgunned.

They were slowly surrounding me, moving like liquid, fanning out in a semicircle. The moonless night and scattered streetlamps made some of them all but invisible in the dark. I did the sensible thing: I ran.

Well, I Walked.

I heard the music box again and a sound like bowling pins toppling over. I smelled something salty and saw a splash of bright pink as I slipped through the In-Between and into yet another version of Greenville.

The street was empty again, but I kept moving anyway, back the way I had come. There was no point in going to Josephine's house, not in that dimension and not in this one. I couldn't sense another version of me here; I didn't know if that was because that version had died, or been captured by Binary or HEX, or if this was the home world of one of my fellow students back on Base. I didn't spend too much time thinking about it.

When I'd expanded my senses to look for Josephine, right before I'd felt HEX's attack, I'd felt her—and she hadn't been home.

What was a version of me, not even seventeen years old, doing away from home at three A.M.? It wasn't like Greenville had an active nightlife (although I suppose this one had a twenty-four-hour diner, at least . . .) and I had never been the most popular of kids. I certainly hadn't been cool enough to hang out with anyone who'd stay out all night. Maybe this version of me was different, but I doubted it.

I kept moving, occasionally hopping into a different dimension to throw off any pursuers. When I'd first started Walking, I'd done it instinctively—and, apparently, badly. One of my teachers had explained that I'd basically punched a hole in the wall instead of finding the door. I'd gotten better at it since then, and it was easier to slip between the worlds without causing as many ripples. I could Walk as many times as there was a portal around; HEX and Binary were operating on borrowed power, so my hope was that being a moving target would discourage them from chasing me too far.

I eventually made my way back to Josephine's Greenville, a few blocks over from where I'd started. The HEX agents didn't seem to be following me anymore; I couldn't sense them when I tried.

I *could* sense her. She was a couple of streets away from where I was now, out of the residential area. I could see the brighter lights of the business district off in the distance, which was definitely where the familiar tug was leading me.

I sighed. Nothing was ever easy. . . .

With my senses on high alert and my ribs aching again from all the movement, I started down the street.

It didn't take me long to track her down, though I was still at a loss as to why she was apparently in an abandoned office building. The hair on the back of my neck was standing on end. The last time I'd been in a place like this, I had found Joaquim, the Walker who'd turned out to not be a Walker at all, who'd betrayed my team and caused Jerzy's death. He'd been pretending to be a captive of Binary so we'd "rescue" him. . . . Had Josephine been taken captive, too?

It was seeming more and more likely. The HEX scouts outside her house . . . maybe they hadn't been waiting for me, after all. Maybe they had found her.

This was bad. I was still running on borrowed time, dealing with several injuries, and had no weapons. I had no one I could call for backup. Josephine was supposed to *become* my backup.

The smart thing to do would be to cut my losses and go—head to another version of Greenville and find another me. Like I said, as long as there were portals, I never had to stop Walking. I could go anywhere I wanted, as long as I got there before FrostNight destroyed everything. . . .

I was berating myself for not ever being able to do the smart thing as I picked the lock on the abandoned building.

See, when HEX and Binary capture a Walker, they don't just kill them. They *use* them. I'd explained that to Mr. Dimas, but I hadn't explained how. HEX boils us down, literally puts us in a giant cauldron, still alive and screaming, and boils us like lobsters. Down past the skin and bones, to our very essence. Then they put that essence in a jar and cast some kind of spell on it and use it whenever they need to Walk. And that's not the worst part, no way.

The worst part is, in some small way, we're still alive. Still *aware*. And we know what's been done to us and what we're being used for.

I'd rather die right now—rather let all the worlds be

destroyed—than allow that to happen to even one more of us.

I stepped through the door, stopping to let my eyes adjust. It had been dark outside, but it was darker in here; the only light that found its way in was through the windows, and most of those were covered with signs saying RENT THIS SPACE.

The floor was marble, one of those nice-looking entry-ways that made you forget you were probably here to see a therapist or dentist. There were doors on either side of me, both closed and sporting tinted-glass windows, and the lobby stretched out into darkness ahead of me.

Everything was silent as I moved, walking carefully across the pristine floor. I listened hard, alert for any sign that I wasn't alone, and a subtle change in air pressure warned me a second before I heard a distinct *click* behind me.

I whirled, going immediately into a crouch, only to discover the figure behind me doing the same.

"Don't move," she hissed, and in her hands was a gun. It was pointed directly at me.

CHAPTER THREE

NOW, I'D SEEN ALL kinds of guns since I started training at InterWorld, from all worlds and times. Blasters, emitters, ray guns, laser guns with detachable Bluetooth scopes, plasma guns, you name it. This was a modern hand-gun, a Colt .45. Basic, easy, and still able to kill me twice before I hit the ground.

"Whoa," I said, holding my hands out in front of me.

"Don't move," she repeated. The gun was leveled at me unwaveringly, and from the look on the face behind it, this wouldn't be its maiden voyage. I wondered if that's how I looked in my weapons training classes. I imagined it wasn't far off, since we shared the same face.

"Josephine," I said, trying to make my voice as soothing as possible. "It's okay. My name is Joe, I'm—"

My words didn't have the calming effect I was hoping for. "It's *you*," she snarled, and her hands began to shake. "You're the one who was in my house that day!"

"Yes," I said, but didn't get any further. She started to stand. So did I, but she gestured me back down with an angry jerk of the gun.

"You ruined my life," she spat, edging closer. I was well versed enough in weapons to know what a bullet from that gun would do to my head if she fired. She was still shaking, though it was obviously from anger rather than fear.

"You don't want to fire that," I said, trying to be reasonable. I hoped she couldn't hear the panic that was threatening to shatter my calm. "The police station isn't too far from here, they'll hear the shots." That was a guess, actually; I remembered that the police station was on a street of the same name as this one, but I had no idea how close or far it was from here.

"I don't care," she said, standing just out of my reach. She was about my height, dressed in loose jeans and a baggy hoodie, both of which looked like they'd seen better days. Her frizzy red hair was short, barely touching her cheeks, and looked like it hadn't been brushed in a while. Despite the baggy clothes, I could see that she was thinner than was healthy. All this added up to a desperation that made me believe her next words. "It'll be worth it. Even if I go to jail, it'll be worth it. They'll finally stop coming after me."

I didn't bother pointing out that if she killed me, it wouldn't matter if she went to jail or not; she'd likely be dead either way when FrostNight destroyed everything. There was something else I could use to make a far better point.

"No, they won't. They aren't after me! Well, they aren't *just* after me. They're after you." The pieces had all fallen together. The HEX agents outside her house had been waiting for *her* to come home. The bad guys had found her because I'd Walked there unknowingly. I'd led them to her.

Simply put, I *had* ruined her life.

"Shut up! You're lying. Why would they be after me? They started coming after you showed up in my house that day. They must be after you!"

"They were, but now they're after *us*. You have to trust me. Look, look at me! We could be twins!"

"You're just one of them, trying to . . . to do whatever weird magic crap they do, to take my place!"

"No, Josephine, listen!" I told her my full name, my birthday, my mother's and father's names and birthdays. I told her where I went to elementary school and what my favorite dessert was. From the look on her face, I could tell everything I said was true for her, too. "If I was trying to take your place, first of all, why would I be a *boy*, and second, why wouldn't I be living your life right now? You're obviously not. You haven't even been home, have you?"

"Not in months," she admitted, though the gun was still pointed at me.

"So why would I come find you?"

"To lead them to me," she said, but she sounded less certain.

"No," I said, as forcefully as I dared. "I'm trying to help you. I *am* you, you from a different world. And you are me, from *this* world."

"And those things?" she asked.

"Those are the bad guys," I said. "I know it's a simple explanation, but we don't have time to get into it. I promise I'll explain on the way, but we can't stay here. They can sense us, and they'll find us eventually. You have to trust me."

She just looked at me, indecision plain on her face. I could almost read every thought as it went through her mind; after all, I knew what I'd be thinking, if I were in her shoes. I knew what I *had* thought, when all of this had first happened to me.

"The alternative is staying here, on your own," I said. "Not being able to go home, not being able to trust *anyone*. I promise, you can trust me."

Her lips twitched, twisting into something halfway between a snarl and a grimace. Her chin trembled, just for a second, and she started to lower the gun.

I heard a faint, cheerful pop behind me, and Josephine's eyes widened. So did mine, as I realized what was going to happen. I shouted, "No, wait!" as she raised her gun and fired, the sound loud enough to temporarily deafen us both.

I darted forward, not even turning to see if Hue was okay.

Josephine was taking aim again. I grabbed her wrist, turning it and jabbing my thumb into the soft tissue below her scaphoid. She dropped the gun, her other hand clenching to a fist, which she swung clumsily at me. She didn't have a quarter of the training I did. I had her in a hold immediately, despite her struggling.

She may not have had my training, but she was definitely used to fighting for her life. She brought a knee up, though not into my groin as I would have expected. Instead, she tried to bring her foot down hard on my instep. I barely avoided it, tightening my grip on her as I looked for Hue.

The little mudluff was bobbing up and down in the air, alternating between a spooked shade of white and a confused blue-gray.

"Hue, are you okay?" I asked, more than a little anxious. I'd once seen him take a laser bolt and come out mostly unscathed, but . . .

"I knew you were one of them," Josephine spat, still struggling.

"I'm not, and neither is Hue. He's a friend of mine, and you almost shot him." The mudluff was spinning slowly, as though to prove to me that he hadn't been hit. I didn't see any marks or discolorations on his surface, which was a small blessing.

"He looks like a demented balloon," she said. "And I've seen weirder from those . . . other things. How was I supposed to know he was a friend of yours? I'm still not sure *you're* a friend of *mine*."

"Well, you'd better get sure," I told her. The slow wail of a siren started up in the distance. I didn't know if someone had called in the gunshot or if it was a coincidence, but I wasn't willing to chance it.

I said as much, letting her go (though I picked up the gun before she could). She stood there uncertainly, alternately watching me and Hue.

"Hue showing up doesn't change anything," I told her, holding the gun nonthreateningly at my side. "You looked like you were about to come with me. If you stay here alone, they *will* catch you. If you come with me—and Hue—they won't. It's that simple." It was too simple, really; I couldn't promise that HEX or Binary would *never* catch her, or that something else wouldn't happen to her, but it was better than leaving her here. I needed her, and she needed me. Us J names had to stick together.

"Come on," I said, and she finally capitulated with poor grace. She growled something that sounded like "fine," and turned to stalk back in through the door she'd surprised me from. I followed.

Through the door was another wide room and an elevator. There was a broom and dustpan leaning up against the wall near the up/down buttons. As I watched, she jabbed the thin part of the dustpan into the slit where the elevator doors met, then pushed until she had enough room to wedge the broom in. Then she pried the doors open, revealing what appeared to be her temporary living area.

She had a ratty-looking sleeping bag and pillow, two beat-up backpacks, and three or four books piled up in the corner of the elevator car. The emergency exit in the roof was propped open, and there was a rope hanging down from it. Honestly, it wasn't a bad setup; all she had to do was take the broom with her when she went out or in, and open the doors barely wide enough for her to slip through so she could get them closed again. She had an emergency exit if anyone did try to come find her, which she could use to get to any floor of the building.

It was exactly what I might have done, if I'd been in her shoes.

She finished stuffing the books into one of the back-packs, and rolled up the sleeping bag before turning to glare at me. The siren was getting louder.

"Now what?" she asked.

"Now," I said, "we go for a Walk."

What I really wanted to do was go straight to InterWorld— the future InterWorld, that is. I haven't explained about that yet, have I? I hadn't said anything about it to Mr. Dimas; there wasn't much point, and I really hadn't wanted to get into the whole time-travel thing. It was messy at best, which was why I'd skimmed over Acacia. I hadn't told him about how I'd been a prisoner of TimeWatch, or how they'd sent me thousands of years into the future to InterWorld. A broken, run-down, destroyed version of InterWorld.

It had been the saddest thing I'd ever seen, and that was saying a lot.

Still, I couldn't get to *my* InterWorld, not now. It was lost in some kind of dimension shift, pursued by a HEX ship. But that other InterWorld, thousands of years in the future . . . I could get back there. Or, more specifically, Hue could.

See, Walkers can't time travel, really. But Hue is, as I've said, a multidimensional life-form—and time, in its own way, is a dimension. TimeWatch had sent me into the future, and Hue had brought me back to the past. That meant he could take me there, again. Me, and Josephine.

That was the part that would take some convincing.

I was explaining all this to her as we sat on a bench in the middle of a park that bore only the slightest resemblance to the one I'd been standing in before; I'd taken a chance and Walked to a farther dimension. If the experience of Walking itself hadn't convinced her, sitting on a bench of green wood under a purple sky watching the blue sunrise probably would. Walking so far had a higher potential to call attention to us, but it also helped to prove my point.

I'd mentioned punching through a wall instead of using a door before, right? Walking without going through the

In-Between was kind of like that. The In-Between was the door; but it was also *crazy*, and I wasn't sure she was ready for it yet. There were some stories among the older Walkers at InterWorld about new recruits who'd gone insane and needed to have their memories wiped after their first trip through the In-Between. I wasn't sure I believed those stories, but why take chances?

"So you can travel through time," she said, watching me like the jury was still out on my sanity.

"I can't," I clarified. "Hue can."

"And he can take us with him."

"Yes."

"To the future."

"Yeah."

"To this 'home base' of yours that was completely destroyed." I nodded. "Why can't he take us *back* in time, to before it got messed up? Or forward to some other time when everyone is okay?"

"It doesn't exactly work like that," I said, but she clearly wanted more explanation. "I think he needs to have something to anchor on," I said, trying to recall everything Acacia had told me about timestreams and anchoring and all that. "Like, he's kind of fixed on me, so he can follow me wherever, even through time. And *I'm* fixed in my personal timestream, so I can only go back and forth within that one."

"That's inconvenient." She looked like she was trying to

figure out whether I was making excuses or not.

"Maybe, but it also stops regular people from messing with time, which could cause all sorts of problems," I said, but an idea was nagging at me. If I *could* go anywhere, if Hue could take me anywhere, would the Time Agents come pick me up? Jay had said they were kind of like law enforcement for the timestreams. . . . If I started messing things up, would that get their attention? Could I get them to help me?

Too risky, I decided, remembering how I'd been treated at the TimeWatch headquarters. They'd kept me in a jail cell and ejected me into the future without a word; I wasn't going to risk letting them do it again. There was too much at stake.

"So you and I are going to go into the future and start recruiting more of us, before the bad guys can use a combination of science and magic to remake the universe," she said, pulling me from my thoughts.

"That's essentially it, yeah."

"And you're saying there are hundreds of us, spread out over every dimension."

"The number is probably incalculable," I said, recalling when I searched for my name in InterWorld's dimensional database. I'd come up with a few thousand matches on my name alone; who knew how many versions of the rest of there were, all with names like Josephine and Jo and Jakon and Josef.

Those last three were teammates of mine. I missed them.

"It's hard to say how many of us there actually are," I continued, pushing aside my sudden melancholy. "Since there are more dimensions being created and destroyed every day. Every second, even. But that's too much to get into right now," I said quickly, seeing her open her mouth to ask. She shut it irritably, her expression heated. "What matters is getting back to the base we've got, getting you and whatever others we can find trained, and stopping FrostNight."

She was staring at me, and I was starting to realize how crazy I sounded. Not just in terms of "You expect me to believe things that sound crazy." Even if you bought everything I was saying about HEX and Binary and time travel and multiple dimensions, even if you decided that was all completely real and sane, I still sounded crazy. My plan was to pick up as many untrained recruits as I could and go head-to-head with the worst baddies in the universe—*both* of them—with no backup or plan B. No matter which way you looked at it, it was both insane and suicidal.

But it was also my only option.

"Okay," she said abruptly. "Let's do it."

I just looked at her.

"What?" she said finally, her tone and posture ratcheting up a notch. "Isn't that the answer you wanted to hear?"

No, I thought unwillingly. To tell the truth, I'd never really thought about whether she'd agree or not. There was never an option in my mind. The plan had been to find Josephine, convince her to help me, take her back to base, then go find all the others and do the same. The fact that she'd agreed to fight in a war she hadn't even known about until five minutes ago made me feel sick, like I was knowingly sending her into a minefield without a map.

In a way, that's exactly what I was doing.

"Yeah," I said, but I don't think she believed me. I know I didn't.

CHAPTER FOUR

GETTING JOSEPHINE TO AGREE to let Hue take us into the future was easier than I thought it would it be. Getting her to actually *do* it, however, was harder.

"No way," she said adamantly, watching the way Hue rippled over my body like a suit of Silly Putty.

"It just feels a little weird," I insisted. "It doesn't hurt."

"I don't care if it feels weird, I don't want that *thing* that close to me."

"His name is Hue," I said, pushing down my temper. "And he's a friend of mine, *and* he's helping us. You don't have to do anything except trust me, okay?"

She fell silent, a muscle twitching in her jaw. She was only willing to trust me so far.

"Look," I said, taking a step closer. Josephine drew back but didn't step away. I held out my hand. After a hesitation that started to grind on my nerves—we didn't have *time* for this—she took it.

Go to her, Hue, I said silently. *Slowly. She's scared.* With Hue wrapped around me like a second skin, I'd found we could communicate without speaking. At least, inasmuch as I could ever communicate with Hue; he seemed to understand basic language (several different ones, in fact), but sometimes there were concepts or nuances that confused him. Or he just ignored me; it was hard to tell.

The Hue putty began to flow down over my arm, toward our hands. I felt her fingers tighten in mine and a resistance like she wanted to pull away, but I held her firmly. Hue moved over our fingers, slowly covering her hand to the wrist. There he stopped, waiting.

"It does feel weird," she said, though she didn't seem as spooked.

"Yeah," I agreed. "Like Silly Putty, right?"

"Like what?"

"Never mind." I sighed. This was a common cultural difference with para-incarnations of myself. Even though both our worlds had McDonald's, there was nothing saying that whoever had invented something like Silly Putty in my world had also done it in hers.

"It's kind of like Putty Dough, I guess," she said.

Close enough. "Sure," I agreed, still holding her hand.

"Now, *trust me*, okay? We're going to do exactly what I said. You have to get closer to me so that Hue can cover us both; he's not that big. Then I'm going to Walk. You'll understand it when you feel it."

"Fine," she said shortly, like she was agreeing before she could change her mind. I stepped forward, putting my arms around her shoulders, while hers settled somewhat hesitantly around my waist.

Honestly, I wasn't really sure how this was going to work. I didn't know if Hue needed to be covering Josephine as well, or if I just needed to be touching her. All I knew was that the chances of something going wrong if she panicked were pretty high, which is why I was holding on to her.

Hue stretched paper-thin over us both, and I felt Josephine press closer against me. It was like being in a sensory-deprivation tank, I would imagine, at least at first. I ceased to feel the air on me, to hear the birds, to see the brightness of the rising blue sun.

And then, as I opened my eyes, I could see and hear and feel *everything.*

Hue was like the universe's best looking glass, like the missing element that made everything fall into place. That made everything make *sense.* Walking was no longer about finding the door, it was about suddenly realizing you were surrounded by doors and you knew exactly where every single one of them went. It was like sitting down at a test you'd never studied for and finding you knew all the answers anyway.

I could feel everything. I could feel Josephine's wonder and terror, her slow understanding and her deep yearning. She was experiencing what she'd been born to do, and I could already feel her fear giving in to eagerness, to the desire to learn.

Even though I theoretically knew where *all* the doors would take me, it's always easiest to go someplace you've already been. I followed the path to future InterWorld flawlessly, and all too soon we were standing there in the purple dawn light, there on that crumbling base.

Josephine let go of me as soon as Hue receded, taking a few steps back, though she didn't look afraid. She looked like she understood.

She walked slowly down the gravel path, alternately staring at the smoke-blackened trees and the scorched ground. I still didn't know what had happened here; perhaps at some point, when I had time, I could have Hue show me.

All I knew was that sometime in InterWorld's future, the base must have been attacked. There were burns all over the place, areas where the ground was dark, rust red with the memory of violence. There was nothing here, not even a breeze. We were alone on a dead world.

"This is the future," Josephine asked, though it didn't sound much like a question.

"Several thousand years from where we were, yeah. I don't know how far exactly," I said, catching sight of something glinting in the morning sun. I knelt to inspect it, finding a twisted scrap of metal that could have been anything from a blaster shell to a piece of jewelry. It wasn't recognizable as anything but junk now.

"So why keep fighting?" she asked.

"What?"

"Why even bother? You said you have to get back to your InterWorld, but it'll just be this eventually. Even if you save it back then, it'll wind up like this." She gestured at the area around us, the shattered glass and dead trees and broken doorways. "You'll lose anyway."

I was silent for a moment, watching Hue float off toward one of the rooftops. He settled there, perched on the edge of it like a balloon-shaped gargoyle, and turned the same color as the metal. I'd never really seen him camouflage before, but the guy had a hundred little tricks I wasn't aware of.

"Yeah, maybe," I said, shoving my hands into the pockets of my sweatshirt. "Eventually."

"So why are you even bothering?"

"Because if I don't, all this"—I shrugged, indicating the devastation around me—"will happen everywhere a lot sooner. There won't even be this left. There won't be any-thing."

She scuffed her foot against the gravel path, watching the

pebbles scatter this way and that. "But doesn't the existence of this ship in the future, even if it's deserted, mean that there *is* a future? That the world doesn't get destroyed?"

"It doesn't work like that," I told her. "FrostNight will erase everything, past, present, and future, all at once. If it's released, this entire dimension, this entire timestream, will all be gone."

She seemed to accept that, though she folded her arms and huddled in on herself, as though she didn't like what she was about to say. "Okay. But, still—let's say you do gather us all up, and we go stop this FrostNight thing. Let's say we save the world, or all the worlds. Why not just let us go home, then?"

I took in a breath, held it for a moment, let it out slowly. "Because InterWorld guards against HEX and Binary. That's what we do. We track their movement, and we thwart them. We make sure they don't get more of us, don't get more weapons. Don't hurt innocent people or take over entire worlds and use the inhabitants for cannon fodder. We're the thorn in their sides, and that's all we can manage. We may not be much, but we're the first line of defense. We're the *only* line of defense. We've gotta keep being that, no matter what. It's all we've got, even if in the end, this is all that's left."

To be honest, I hadn't really been sure what I was going to say when I opened my mouth. The words had just come to me, based on a bunch of different things, mostly stuff I'd heard the Old Man say. He wasn't a man of many words, but the ones he did use tended to be pretty effective.

Josephine was looking at me with her eyes narrowed, like she still wasn't sure what my game was. "I still think you're crazy," she said, "but now it's for different reasons."

"Yeah," I said, and turned to walk into the base. After a moment, I heard her follow me.

"First order of business is to get to the control room," I told her as we picked our way through the debris in the hallways. "There might still be some auxiliary power cores laying around. I have no idea when this happened, so I don't know if they'll still be good."

"What if they're not?"

"Then we hope they can be recharged."

"Recharged? How?"

"That depends on how old they are," I explained, shoving down my rising impatience. I had nothing to do but explain things as we made our way to the control room, and she really didn't know any of this. I imagine I was much the same when Jay had first picked me up. "They can be charged a few different ways, if the transducers are still working. Thermal energy, chemical, electromagnetic, etc. The ship mostly runs on kinetic energy, as I understand it." I glanced back to see if she was following all this, then elaborated. "Meaning, once it gets started, it'll work up its own momentum and charge itself."

"I see," she said, climbing her way over a pile of rubble. "So how do you get it started?"

"Well, some kind of pulse. A shock, or—"

"Like a static shock?"

"It'd have to be more powerful than that, but that's the right idea."

"So if the trans . . . ducers aren't working?"

"We fix them somehow."

"How?"

"I don't know how," I admitted. "So let's hope they're working."

"Okay," she said, sounding dubious. I could practically hear her second-guessing her decision to come with me, as I obviously didn't know what I was doing.

She was pretty much right.

It didn't take long for us to make our way to the control room. I was anxious every step of the way; I kept expecting to run into bad guys, or worse—what was left of the good guys. There was nothing, though, no bodies of any kind or evidence of anything living. On the one hand, I was glad. On the other, I wanted to know what had happened here. I wanted to know how to stop it.

We did find some used-up power cores, and some of them still had juice. Not enough to get the ship up and running but enough to give us a boost for the mechanisms that still worked. Such as activating the solar panels.

"At least we'll have some power once the sun rises over-head," I said, flipping a long line of switches that activated the panels all over the roof of the main building.

"So this is both a ship and a town, sort of," Josephine observed, carefully watching what I was doing.

"Yeah. The whole thing is a ship—it just doesn't *look* like one. It doesn't look enclosed, but it is. At least, it is when the shields are working, so we can phase to worlds that don't have the right kind of air for us."

"But this world does, right?"

"Obviously, or we wouldn't be breathing."

"How did you know it would?"

"I've been here before. The ship can't phase without the engines, and the engines don't run without power. I knew it'd be in the same place."

"So we can phase again if we get power?"

"Maybe. I know power makes the ship run, but I don't know exactly how we make it phase. I know how HEX and Binary do it with *their* ships, but . . ." I shook my head. That wasn't on the table.

"How?" I should have seen that question coming.

"They use us," I said as bluntly as I could to keep from discussing it further. "They take our ability to Walk and use it for their own ships."

She pressed her lips together, looking away. Even as new

to this as she was, she knew what it was like to Walk, and I think she already couldn't imagine having that taken away. I knew how she felt.

"Come on," I said, flipping one final switch. "It's time for a lesson."

I hadn't really bothered looking out any windows the last time I was here. I'd been in too much of a hurry, too desperate to get back to where I belonged. Back then, I'd assumed the ship was still floating above the ground, cruising along at about five thousand feet as usual.

I'd realized it slowly as we made our way through the ship this time, but we were actually docked: completely and utterly still. We were sitting on the ground in a wide-open field, nothing but grassy plains visible as far as the eye could see. There might have been a sparkle of water in the distance, but it could just as easily have been a trick of the light.

"Are we alone on the planet, too?" Josephine asked, once she'd taken in the size of InterWorld itself. We weren't talking the size of New York or anything, but it certainly would have taken a while to walk all the way around it.

"Depends on your definition," I said, pointing to a group of butterflies collecting around some flowers. "We're the only people. This is a prehistoric world."

"But I thought we were in the future."

I paused. *Oh, boy. This is about to get complicated.* "We are. But InterWorld operates on a broad spectrum of locations.

Not just back and forth"—I moved my hand from side to side—"but forward and backward. There are thousands of different dimensions programmed into the soliton array engines, but only three basic Earths. The ship moves—or moved—forward and backward in time over a certain period, as well as sideways into different dimensions on those three Earths. Even though the ship *can* move further into the future, we tend to stay in prehistoric times and move sideways. Less chance of startling the locals that way."

She was glaring at me. "Did you actually answer my question, or did you just spout a bunch of bull—"

"Sorry, sorry. I got carried away. Basically, *we* are not in the future. We're in the past, because that was the last place this InterWorld docked. But *this* InterWorld came here, to the past of this world, from the future."

She frowned, considering. "But . . . we went into the future. Sort of. I mean, that's what it felt like. It was like taking a giant step forward, when your bubble thing—"

"Hue."

"—was wrapped around us."

"Yes, but we went forward into InterWorld's future, which took us to the past," I explained. "So the ship is from the future, but the planet is in the past. Make sense?"

She hesitated, looking like she had a question that she thought might be considered stupid. After a moment, she asked, "Are there dinosaurs here?"

I didn't laugh. I kind of wanted to, but I understood why she was asking. I mean, wouldn't you have? I know *I* would have. "I honestly don't know," I told her, and she glanced around as though she might see one. "On some planets, yes, there are. And, yes," I said, unable to help a grin, "I've seen them. But I don't know if it's this one. I don't know which planet we parked on."

"Okay," she said, still looking up at the sky, which was brightening to a blinding blue. It was chilly out here in the early morning, but we both had our sweatshirts on, and the sun was warm where it was rising over the horizon. "So what now?"

"Now I teach you to Walk," I said, gesturing for her to follow me. "You want to be away from everything for your first try. It's really difficult to Walk into something that's already there, but it's not impossible."

"You mean, I could get stuck in a rock, or something . . . ?"

"Like I said, it's unlikely, but it *is* possible. We've basically got built-in subliminal algorithms for that kind of thing, like an instinctive navigational system. Reflex, kinda. But when you're first learning, it's better not to take any chances."

"Okay," she said, watching me closely. She had a familiar look of determination on her face; familiar, because she looked so much like me. "Teach me."

I spent the better part of the afternoon teaching her how to Walk, and discovered that not only was she a fantastic student, she had a particular ability for it. Not that it came easier to her than to any of the rest of us (in fact, it took her the better part of an hour to follow my instructions correctly), but once she learned it, she slipped through the dimensions like a cat burglar on an easy heist. I even lost her once, which was a frightening moment, considering she was my only recruit. I wound up having to sidestep through four different dimensions and cast my senses about for her every time, which was more than a little tiring.

"And you've never Walked before?" I asked once I'd found her, sitting in the middle of the field, blowing tufts of dandelions into the wind.

"Never before today," she said, looking pleased with herself. "Why?"

"Well, you're pretty good at it," I said, readjusting the brace strapped around my wrist. I'd had an itch there I'd been trying to ignore for the past fifteen minutes.

"I thought it was taking me a while to learn."

"It took you a while to get it, maybe, but once you did . . . You're almost undetectable, you know that?"

"Yeah?" she asked, looking up at me. She didn't look guarded anymore or angry or like she was about to run. She looked happy, the way I remembered my sister looking when she was having nice dreams. Content. Peaceful.

"Yeah. It's like when you step into the water, you don't make any ripples. You just sort of slip in."

She smiled and shrugged, though I could tell she was pleased to be good at something in particular. I know I would have been.

"Will that be helpful?" she asked.

"Yes," I told her honestly, offering my noninjured left hand. She took it, allowing me to pull her to her feet. "If you do the Walking, we'll be able to gather up the others without being detected. Gives us a lot more breathing room. Why don't you give it a try now? Walk back to the world we parked on."

Usually, when teaching a new Walker how to get back to base, they're taught a formula. It's an address, an equation that tells us exactly how to get home, wherever home happened to be. It tells us that no matter where the base is, we are connected to it, and we can find it anywhere.

This future InterWorld—InterWorld Beta, as I'd come to think of it—might or might not have the same address, when it was powered on. Since it wasn't currently on, I had no way of knowing; I just knew that the address *I* knew, the one for what would be InterWorld Alpha, was a dead end. Maybe it wouldn't be if the ship ever stopped, or if it turned out the address could be used for InterWorld Beta when the ship powered up again. Either way, it was useless; there was no reason to teach it to her now.

Josephine kept hold of my hand, closing her eyes and focusing. I kept mine open; it was easier to Walk when you weren't watching your surroundings change around you, but I was just along for the ride this time.

The scenery shifted; we were standing in shadows one moment, then again in sunlight.

A flock of birds passed above our heads. . . .

The ground trembled beneath us for a moment, as though a herd of something large was stampeding nearby. . . .

The brief, salty scent of the ocean and the cry of a seagull from over the mountains . . .

And then InterWorld Beta rested in front of us, sad and majestic, like a ship run aground. An abandoned city lost to time.

Josephine kept hold of my hand this time, as the world settled back around us. It was lonely, somehow. It was our salvation and our hope; it was part of what let us witness the extraordinary things we'd seen and experience the amazing things we'd done. It was the wind in our hair and the travel dust on our boots, and it wasn't right for it to be stuck here, dead and lifeless.

She looked at me, subdued and determined, and let go of my hand. We had an understanding, then, and I think she finally knew why I was willing to risk everything. I think she was willing to, as well.

It was a small comfort, at least.

CHAPTER FIVE

WE RAIDED THE STOREROOM, gathering anything and everything that might be helpful. We brought cleaning supplies as well as thick gloves and kneepads into the hallways, and we spent the rest of the morning clearing out the debris and making sure there were easy paths to get to the main places we needed to go.

From the control room to the storeroom, down to the lower decks where we could get out onto our temporary home planet, to the living quarters, the mess hall, and back up to the control room. It took until well into the afternoon, and we were starving despite the few snacks and energy bars we'd taken from our backpacks.

The mess hall hadn't yielded much in the way of food, not even the protein packs or MREs I was used to. The only thing I found of any use was a few gallons of water stored away in still-sealed containers, which were admittedly *very* useful. We poured several of them into the septic filtration system, which was completely empty. I didn't know if any remaining liquid had simply dried up, or if it had been emptied on purpose. For all I knew, this could have been a base-wide evacuation.

"I can Walk somewhere and get food," Josephine suggested, as we were sorting through a stack of discarded electronics in an attempt to find anything helpful. I hesitated. On the one hand, she had already demonstrated her ability to Walk without causing so much as a ripple and would most likely be able to go get us supplies without incident.

On the other hand, she was all I had.

"I'm not sure that's a good idea," I said, and was rewarded with a disgusted look.

"What are we going to eat, then?"

"I can go get something," I said, but she shook her head.

"You've gotta start trusting me sometime," she said. "I can't be the only one taking leaps of faith here."

"It's not about trust," I protested. "You're my first and only recruit. You're my responsibility. I can't let you run off to do something potentially dangerous, and beyond that, where are you even going to go? We're on a prehistoric Earth, remember? It's not like you can just Walk to the corner store and buy us some milk."

Now it was her turn to hesitate, though it was for an admirably short moment. "There are other ways to get food.

I'm sure there are fruit trees, right? And fish?"

"I don't think there are fish trees," I said, and she threw a coil of copper wire at me. I'd gotten her to laugh, though. Sort of. "Although, that's not a bad idea. Fishing, I mean."

"No, it's not. I don't even have to Walk anywhere, I can just go off ship. Okay? Send your bubble thing to find me if I'm taking too long."

"His name is Hue," I reminded her, though I refrained from pointing out that I wasn't sure I could really *send* Hue anywhere. He wasn't exactly at my beck and call.

"Whatever. Gimme one of those satchels and I'll go get us some fruit, okay? It's better than nothing, which is what we've got."

I handed her one. Somewhat reluctantly, but I knew she was right; I had to start trusting her. We'd only been working together for a few hours, but this was fate-of-the-world stuff. I needed to let her stretch her legs, and it was best she do it now while we were still relatively safe.

Besides, this meant *I* could do a few things around the ship I was way more comfortable doing on my own.

First and foremost, once she left, I made my way down the cleared hallways to the living quarters. It may have been silly, but I wanted to find my own room—or what had been my room. If this InterWorld was thousands of years in the future, I'm sure I was long dead. It must belong to another Walker by now, but I just . . . wanted to see. I wanted something to be familiar, anything at all.

Nothing was, of course. InterWorld didn't allow for much customization in the first place, and whoever had used this room before the base was evacuated (abandoned? Surrendered?) hadn't left any personal items. The most I found was an old T-shirt, so yellowed with age that it was impossible to tell whether it had ever had any kind of logo on it at all.

I set my backpack in there nevertheless, and swept out as much of the dust as I could. The shift shutters—made of the thick acrylic they use to make airplane windows—were down and wouldn't open until the ship was powered again. The sun had been up for a few hours now, and was currently directly overhead; the solar panels were soaking it in, and with any luck we would have enough power to run basic functions by the time Josephine got back. Then I could open the windows and air out the rooms, get the dust out of the ventilation systems, use the stove and ovens in the kitchen, and (I hoped) have enough hot water for a shower.

And maybe, if I could use the solar energy to charge a few of the power cores, I could get the Hazard Zone up and running. Then Josephine would have a chance to *really* stretch her legs.

She came back a few hours later, right as I was starting to worry. While she was gone, I'd managed to get two rooms as cleaned out as I could for us, and moved our stuff into both of them. I was staying in "my" room; hers was right next door. I figured it'd be safe enough and far less awkward than trying to share. I was still pretty sure she didn't like me much. That was sort of par for the course with most of my para-incarnations, it seemed. (A small part of me wondered exactly what psychological implications it had that I never seemed to particularly like myself. The rest of me was just concerned with trying to keep everyone alive.)

I'd also managed to start up the ventilation system, and there'd been enough solar power to get the shift shutters open by the time Josephine got back. We'd still pretty much be inhaling centuries of dust for a while, but it wouldn't be as bad tomorrow.

"These apples are as big as your head," Josephine said once she'd found me again, tossing one in my direction. I caught it reflexively, though it took both hands. She wasn't kidding.

"Good," I said, taking a bite. "More for . . ." I paused, chewing slowly. "It doesn't taste like an apple."

"Is it bad?" She eyed her own suspiciously.

"No, it just . . . doesn't taste like an apple. It's good, though."

She took a bite. "It kind of tastes like an apple. Like . . . a weird apple."

"The Evolution of Apples," I said, putting a note of drama in my voice. It was supposed to be funny, but she paused and looked down at the giant red fruit in her hands.

"Y'know, we're probably eating something no one has eaten for thousands of years," she said.

"Millions," I corrected. "But, yeah. It's one of the perks of this job." She tried not to look pleased, but I could tell she was. We ate our giant not-apples in silence.

"Okay, boss," she said, once we were finished eating and had found homes in the kitchen for the various other fruits, vegetables, nuts, and berries she'd brought back. "What now?"

"Now," I said, glancing outside at the sky. "We take our much-deserved hot showers while we still have solar power, and go to sleep."

As pleased as she looked at the notion of a hot shower, she looked equally disappointed that it was bedtime so soon. "Aren't you tired?" I asked, abruptly feeling like I was talking to a small child.

"No," she said, looking like she meant it. "I want to learn more."

"Well, I've been up since three this morning, and it hasn't exactly been a restful day. I'm falling over. You can entertain yourself if you want, but I would advise you to get some sleep. I'll likely be up between four and five again, and I'm waking you up with me."

"Fine." She shrugged. "Can I really entertain myself? Like . . . can I explore?"

"I'd prefer you didn't," I said, warily. "But I won't tell you not to. Just stay on the ship, okay?"

She hesitated, but nodded. "Okay."

"Fine. I'm going to go enjoy my shower."

"Where are they? I'll want one later."

"You've got a small bathroom in your room. Let me show you where it is."

I led her back to the rooms (she seemed pleased that I'd already moved her stuff in there, or possibly that we wouldn't be sharing), and showed her how to use all the facilities, as they were built to be compact and were more complicated than the turn of a knob. Despite her excitement at the idea of exploring the ship, I heard her puttering around in the adjacent room as I went about getting ready for sleep. I guess she was glad for the space, since she'd been living in an elevator. Not that our rooms were *that* much bigger, but still . . . bigger than an elevator, even a large corporate one.

All in all, the day hadn't gone too badly. I was still sore, hungry, exhausted, and terrified that the universe might end at any moment—but I had a ship, a recruit, and a plan. It was more than I'd had yesterday.

For the next three days, Josephine and I stuck to a specific routine. We would wake up at five, go for a jog around the ship (which was torture for my injuries at first, but slowly got easier), come in and eat breakfast, then clear out and organize until lunch. Then we would go out again, to a stream about two miles away (we jogged), where I taught her to catch fish with her bare hands. I was glad once again for my Inter-World classes; though such happenings were rare, we had all gone through basic wilderness survival courses in case we ever ended up stranded on a primitive world.

As I stood knee-deep in the stream, showing her how the light bent in the water and made the fish seem slightly to the side of where they actually were, I remembered how much trouble J'r'ohoho had always had with this lesson. The centaur hadn't been able to bend over as far as the rest of us had and couldn't even reach the water without wading in deeper. His hooves kept slipping on the slick rocks, and he'd ended up soaking wet with only a single fish to show for it.

Josephine did well, catching her first fish on her fourth try. She lost it again as it wriggled out of her grasp, but was able to hold on to the second and third. She did better and better as the days went on, and I took to giving her a crash course in battlefield tactics while we brought the fish back to base. Learning how to anticipate the enemy was discussed while we got our catch cleaned and cooked; then, while we ate, I explained the basics of planar travel and the concept of *why* Walking worked.

After lunch, we'd go for another run around the base, then I'd give her combat training. She had a better chance against me than she thought she did, with all my injuries, but I still managed to teach her some basics without hurting myself further. Then it was more cleaning out and hauling (specifically the other dorm rooms) and more combat tactics, specifically in regard to what she could expect from HEX and Binary. A final jog around the base, more fish for dinner, then an hour of leisure time before bed.

The first and second day, she used that extra hour to sleep. The third day, looking no less exhausted but even more determined, she asked me for another lesson in combat.

The fourth day, I decided it was time.

"Hue will bond with us again," I explained, "and we'll go back to our proper timeline. Then, through Hue, I'll search for another Walker. I'll go with you on this first one, but eventually, you and I will be running separate extraction teams."

"Meaning we'll both go after different versions of us."

"Yes."

For the first time in three days, she looked pensive. "How am I supposed to just . . . pull another one of me out of their life? It's not fair."

"The same way I did it to you," I told her.

She frowned. "You didn't give me a choice—you showed up and things started coming after me. . . ."

"Exactly. I didn't give you a choice." It was harsh, but it was true. It had to be true. It was the only way we could win.

She glared down at her shoes for a moment, then nodded. "Okay." After a pause, her expression relaxed, though she still didn't smile. "I'm sick of fish, anyway."

"Me, too." I put a note of sympathy in my voice, sort of as an apology for my tone a moment ago.

"Are we going now?" she asked.

"Now's as good a time as any," I said, but the reality was that now was when Hue happened to be here (we hadn't seen him at all for the past three days), and I didn't want to chance his disappearing again for longer this time. She nodded.

"Hue?" I called, and the little mudluff perked up from where he'd been doing a passable impression of a floor mat. He rose slowly, like a balloon being filled with helium, and floated over. "Hey, buddy," I said, reaching out to touch a hand to his side. He turned a pleased powder blue, exerting slight pressure against my palm. "You ready?" He shifted color again, this time to an affirmative bronze, and I reached out for Josephine's hand.

As before, Hue flowed over us both like weird, nonsticky honey, and I Walked.

Josephine was a bit more used to Walking now, which made the transition smoother for me; but we were stumbling along the path rather than gliding, the gait of a weary traveler who has been on their feet for far too long.

I think Hue is getting tired, Josephine thought at me. Well, it wasn't really *thinking* at me, exactly; it was more that I was aware of her thoughts. Like she was saying them out loud, even though I knew she wasn't.

Probably, I answered. *I don't know how much this takes out of him, but he's been sleeping a lot.*

Let's try not to make so many trips, she suggested. *We can Walk side to side and gather up as many Walkers as we can find, then take them back all at once.*

It wasn't a bad plan, and if I had Josephine do most of the side-to-side Walking—meaning we'd go from dimension to dimension rather than back and forth through time—there was far less chance of us being detected. I had to make these next few trips count.

With that in mind, I cast about for the strongest source of Walker energy I could find.

And I found it. *Close.*

Well, relatively speaking. We had been docked on one of the prehistoric Earths in InterWorld's future. Hue took us back in InterWorld's timeline, which took us forward in Earth's timeline. The Walker essence I was sensing was on a parallel planet, an Earth that had never recovered from the meteor impact roughly sixty-six million years ago.

The energy I was sensing on this planet, this dead planet, was *strong.* Very strong.

Could it be a trap? Josephine asked silently.

A few days ago, I would have said no. I would have said there was no way to simulate Walker energy from someone who wasn't a Walker. I would have said we would *know.*

I knew now that wasn't true, so all I said was *Maybe.*

The landing sent a jolt through us both, like when you're going downstairs and hit the floor sooner than you expected because you thought there was another step. The ground was hard and unforgiving, reddish, and cracked like a dry river-bed. The air was thick with dust and ash, the sunlight filtering weakly through the haze. It smelled like rot and marshland, the landscape restricted to a color palette of grays and reds and browns. Despite the warm colors, it was freezing.

"Ugh." Josephine wheezed, lifting her sleeve to her mouth and nose. "It smells like bad water."

"Yep," I said, doing the same. "Hold on." I closed my eyes, partly to concentrate and partly because they were sting-ing and watering. Taking a deep breath through my sleeve, I focused on the strong, clear pulse of familiarity, of power just like mine, the same way I'd found Josephine. It was here, still, laid out before me like a trail of bread crumbs.

"This way," I said, starting off through the trees. Jose-phine followed, coughing.

"This dust is really thick," she observed, voice muffled by her sleeve. "Did a volcano explode or something?"

I ignored the jolt of adrenaline that went through me as her question reminded me of the rockslide that had killed Jerzy and fractured my shoulder. I wanted to stop and take a deep breath, but that wasn't really an option. Instead, I shrugged and said, "Maybe. More likely it was a huge meteor."

"You mean like what killed the dinosaurs?"

"Yeah. This is a version of Earth that suffered longer-lasting effects from that, whatever it was."

"You just said it was a huge meteor."

"That's what it probably was," I said. "But no one really knows for sure. Evidence suggests it was a meteor, but scientists have a few other theories."

She tilted her head, looking curious. "Aren't those things we could find out, though? Like if it *was* a meteor and whether or not there was an Atlantis, and what's up with the Bermuda Star, and . . ."

"There's actually nothing up with the Bermuda Star," I said. "It's called the Bermuda Triangle on my world, and it's mostly a myth perpetuated by television and other media."

"But all those planes and ships went missing," she said, looking disappointed.

"Not really. There haven't actually been any more disappearances or wrecks in that area than any other," I said. She continued to look disappointed. "I mean, at least on my Earth. Maybe it's different on yours."

"Maybe," she said, perking up. "But what about the other stuff, like Atlantis or the missing crew of the *Maria Christine*?"

"I haven't heard of that last one—might've had a different name on my world, if it happened—but the fact that you and I both come from a world with Atlantis myths might mean there's something to them."

"Huh." She looked thoughtful. "I guess so. Would that be another way of finding out, do you think? Walking to different worlds and seeing if they have the same myths, or finding one where Atlantis never sank?"

"Yeah, probably. And that," I said, removing my sleeve from my face long enough for her to see me grin, "is what we call perks of the job. We do get to go off Base sometimes."

"That's awesome," she said. "I can't wait to explore."

"When we're done saving all the worlds," I reminded her.

"I know," she said a little testily. I suppose I didn't have to keep reminding her how serious this was; there wasn't anything wrong with looking forward to dessert while knowing you still had to eat your vegetables.

"I used to have a whole book about stuff like that," I said after a moment, trying to make conversation as we slogged our way through the thick, dank air. I knew I should save my breath, but we hadn't had much chance to talk about anything other than tactics and technical ship stuff. I knew next to nothing about her, except what I assumed we had in common.

"Stuff like what? Modern mysteries?"

"Yeah. My aunt gave it to me."

"I had the same one," she said. "Aunt Theresa?"

"Yeah." I smiled. "Blue cover?"

"No, green. Yellow title."

"Mine was black, I think. Don't remember; I got it when I

was really little. Mom and her sister didn't talk much, really."

"I guess that's how it was for us at first, but they got closer after the accident," she said.

"What accident?"

"The car accident." Josephine glanced sidelong at me. "When Mom lost her arm."

I paused, once again struck by the realization at how different we all were, even though we were all essentially the same. When I'd first come to Josephine's world, when I still didn't know what was happening or why, I'd gone into her house and seen the woman who was my mom but wasn't, who looked like her and sounded like her but had different hair and a prosthetic arm.

"That didn't happen for you," she said.

"No," I admitted. "I remember one car accident we were in, but it wasn't bad."

She was silent for a moment, considering that. She didn't seem upset, just thoughtful. Josephine was like that, I was learning; she tended to mostly roll with the punches. I guess she'd had to.

"Well, it was bad for us. I have a scar right here from when I hit my head." She pulled her sleeve away from her mouth long enough to push her hair back. I couldn't make out the scar with how my eyes were watering from the dust in the air, but I nodded anyway. "And I only sort of remember what happened. I woke up in the hospital with Dad sitting next to me, and he told me we'd be staying there for a few days while Mom had surgery."

"I'm sorry," I said, unable to think of anything else.

"Whatever," she said. "Don't pity me or anything. It wasn't that bad. Mom's used to using the prosthetic now, and she can do most things pretty easily. She even makes jewelry."

I automatically reached up to touch the necklace beneath my shirt, the one I always wore. My mom had made it for me the night I left home, and I wondered if Josephine's mother had been able to do the same before she left.

"Is it just me, or is it getting harder to breathe?" she asked.

"It's not just you," I said, pausing. "And do you hear that?"

We both stopped, holding our breaths for more than one reason. Had I heard a faint rustling nearby? Now I wasn't sure. There was the same unnatural stillness that had surrounded us since we arrived: no birds, no breeze, no insects. But now there was a heaviness to the air, a sense of *waiting*, of anticipation.

I tackled Josephine to the side as I felt the ground shudder behind me and slightly to the right, my only indication that something was about to happen. I felt a rush of air over my head, and heard a shrill, strangled sound that made my spine tingle. It sounded almost like a bird, but . . . not.

I rolled defensively to my feet, some small part of me noting with pride that Josephine was doing the same.

A shape loomed up out of the red dust at us, beady eyes glinting in the scant light. It looked like some sort of ostrich or emu, but . . . well, not nearly as silly. Large, flightless birds have always looked kinda weird to me, you know? Not this one. For one thing, it was probably close to twice my height, and I know I'm not exactly big, but *still*.

I rolled to the side again as the thing's head—almost the size of my torso—lunged toward me, fast as a striking snake. I got the impression of some kind of hooked beak before it spun past me, orienting on Josephine. Definitely carnivorous, definitely hungry.

I'd like to say what I did next was heroic, but it was probably closer to dumb. As Josephine darted backward to avoid the beak, I threw myself toward the thing in what I hoped was a coordinated jump. It probably looked more like I was flailing while falling, but I managed to get my arms around the thing's long neck anyway, legs wrapped around its body and feet off the ground.

It's times like that, half-astride the back of a prehistoric monstrous emu, that I wondered what I'd be doing right now if my life was normal. Probably not playing rodeo with a giant bird, that's for sure.

"Run!" I shouted, scrabbling for purchase as the whatever it was hopped and bucked. I managed to get an arm around its neck, locking my grip with my other hand. I felt feathers and rough, leathery skin against my arm, and then

I felt my teeth rattle as it tried to run me into a tree. Basic anatomy teaches that most mammal or avian creatures have to breathe, usually through a windpipe of some sort, and I was hoping this thing would be no different. Of course, with all the soot and dust down here, I might have been way off the mark. . . . Maybe this creature had evolved to not need oxygen? I probably should have considered that sooner.

Out of the corner of my eye I saw Josephine tuck and roll, lashing out with a well-placed kick against the joint of one leg. The creature tipped beneath me and I lost purchase, swinging around in front of it. This was not ideal, as now it was able to dip its head enough that the beak had once again become a concern.

I did the smart thing and let go, managing to land more or less neatly on both feet. Josephine dove behind a tree as the creature struck—there was the sound of snapping twigs and creaking bark as the razor-sharp beak left a small crater in the trunk. I had no doubt that beak could snap my arm in half, if it caught me.

I was sorting through my mental index of potential weapons when I heard another sound, this one the piercing cry of something much larger. A shadow passed over us, blotting out what little sun there was, and the giant bird thing paused, lifting its head. I saw the pupils of its eyes contract to pinpoints; then it stood up to its full height and let out a challenging shriek. As it did, I noticed the distinct lines of ribs beneath its feathery coat—whatever it was, it was clearly starving. Either there wasn't much food here, or this thing wasn't high enough on the food chain to compete. If the latter was true, I didn't want to stick around to find out what *was*.

I made it around Josephine's tree just in time to see something large and sinewy crash through the forest, talons out. It was maybe the size of a small airplane.

Nope, I thought, and grabbed Josephine's hand. There was no way we could fight these things; I had nothing on me except Hue, who was resting in the hood of my sweatshirt—and he was no match for monsters like these, anyway. Josephine was already moving, and we took off through the underbrush as fast as we could safely go, given the fact that we couldn't see more than six feet in front of us.

In retrospect, we probably should have gone even slower. The crashing and sounds of fighting were still all too close behind us when the dirt beneath my feet loosened, and I realized we were going downhill, fast. Despite my best efforts, my feet slid out from under me and I stumbled down the rocky ravine, Josephine beside me.

For a single terrifying moment, my shoes left the dirt and I was midair, with no idea of how far I might be falling. Then the ground caught me, not too gently; the wind got knocked out of me and I stayed there for a moment, stunned and in pain. The adrenaline caught up with me a second later, and

I shoved my sleeve back up against my mouth, sucking in breaths only partially filtered of dust. I could hear Josephine coughing beside me, but it was all I could do to concentrate on breathing, on not panicking that I wasn't getting enough air.

This place is a deathtrap, I thought, dizzily. *How is there such a strong source of Walker energy here?*

"Are we sure . . . this is the right . . . place?" Josephine wheezed, voice muffled behind her hands.

"Yes." I coughed. "Well, I'm not sure *this* is the right place, since *this* seems to be some sort of deep . . . ravine. . . ." I paused. Josephine turned to look at me, expression both wary and weary. "Do you hear that?" I asked, feeling my shoulders slump. I was really tired of things trying to kill/maim/eat me.

Josephine tilted her head, listening. By the frown on her face, I could tell she heard it, too—a kind of clicking, or scrabbling, like something with a lot of legs crawling over rocks . . . or many somethings with a lot of legs. . . .

"Nope," Josephine said, covering her ears with her hands. "Nope, I don't hear anyth—"

"Come on!" I took off down the ravine floor, dodging rocks the size of my head and thin, spindly plants that looked like they'd either crumble to dust as I passed or be as strong and tough as razor wire.

Josephine was a few steps behind me. The sound was rising into an all-out chittering, and I didn't dare look back as I ran. Only six feet of vision in this dust, remember?

Yeah. About that . . .

"Dead end!" Josephine gasped, removing her sleeve from her mouth long enough to press her hands against the rocks. There was a sheer cliff face in front of us, rising farther than I could see. I turned around.

I couldn't see anything yet, but the noise was getting closer. As I watched, narrowing my eyes to try to see through the dust and resulting tears, I caught a glimpse of movement here and there at the edges of my vision. Long, sinewy black things, winding like snakes and skittering like scorpions. I started to make out a snap-snap-snap sound, like powerful little claws.

"Climb!" I said, cupping my hands and bracing myself to help Josephine up. She looked at me, at the cliff, and back toward the crab-snake-scorpion creatures. "See how high up it is!" I urged, remembering her reluctance to leave when I'd told her to run from the emu thing. She really wasn't one to back down from something, even when it was probably safer for her. I'd have to keep that in mind.

She put her foot into my cupped hands and I heaved, ignoring the pain in my shoulder and ribs. It was definitely gonna be time for some painkillers once everything on this planet stopped trying to murder us.

I backed up against the cliff, once again trying to figure out what I could use as a weapon. The black shapes were getting closer, taking their time now to assess my threat level. I tried to make myself look as big as possible.

They were about two feet long each, more like centipedes than snakes, with a bunch of spindly black legs, crablike claws, and a wicked, scorpion-like tail. Now that they were closer, I could see there were patterns on their bodies, threads of red and blue and gold winding around their scales (carapaces?). It was kind of pretty, or it would be if they weren't probably about to eat me.

"I'm up, it's not that far!" Josephine called, and I took a breath and turned my back to them. I could barely see the outline of Josephine leaning over the cliff face, offering me her hand. I jumped and grabbed it with my good arm, using my feet and other hand for purchase as something wrapped around my leg.

I kicked wildly, feeling a crunch between my knee and the cliff face as Josephine hauled me up. Rocks and sticks dug into my hands and fingers as I scrambled over the precipice, but I pushed myself immediately to my feet and backed away from the cliff. I didn't know if those creatures could climb or not, but it was probably safer to assume they could.

Josephine pressed her back to mine and we stood like that, panting, me facing the cliff and watching for any sign of those little spindly nightmare things, and Josephine facing wherever we were and looking for who knows what else. Giant emus. Demonic Big Bird, maybe, or a freaking tyrannosaur.

With our luck, the one T. rex not extinct would live on this rock.

"Are you *sure* this is the right planet?" Josephine grumbled, finally, after a moment of blessed silence when nothing came up over the cliff edge or attacked us from the thick dust.

"Yes." I sighed. "Hey, do you—"

"If you say 'Do you hear that?' I *swear* I will shoot you!"

I almost wanted to laugh, but I didn't have the breath for it. "Do you have a handkerchief?"

"Are you kidding me?" she asked. "Who carries a handkerchief anymore?"

"Everyone on InterWorld," I defended myself. "They're useful for a bunch of reasons. Like tying them around your face to block out smoke."

"Well, I don't," she snapped, then reconsidered. "I have a bandanna and a knife. We could cut it in half."

"Better than nothing," I said.

It didn't take long to slice Josephine's blue bandanna in half diagonally, to use as a face mask for each of us. I pulled a water bottle out of my backpack, took several gulps, gave it to Josephine, and soaked both rags before tying mine around my mouth and nose. I automatically put the empty plastic bottle back in my pack so as not to litter, then had to laugh at myself. We were all taught to leave as little imprint on the worlds we visited as possible, so of course I would put the bottle away—but the thought of someone ever coming to this dead planet and finding a single plastic water bottle amid all the ruin was suddenly absurdly funny. I think I was a little hysterical.

I found Josephine's hand, forging ahead through the cloud of dust and debris. There were boulders rather than trees now, giant black rocks bigger than I was, blocking the way. In some cases we had to go around, and the rocks reminded me of the last time I'd breathed in this much dust. This was like when I'd fractured my shoulder in the rockslide that had killed Jerzy.

I felt myself tensing up, expecting the ground to start rumbling and the boulders to start falling, to crush us. My heart was racing, but I didn't know if it was the lack of oxygen or the sudden onslaught of memories. Either way, as Josephine and I plodded on, it took me a moment to notice the figure stepping out of the dust in front of us.

Josephine gave a sharp tug on my hand, which caused pain in about four different places. I snapped my head up, shifting my weight to my back foot—and then the air cleared, so suddenly it left me gasping.

Josephine's hand slipped free of mine, likely so she could wipe her eyes. I didn't blame her; I was doing the same.

"You're Joseph Harker, aren't you?" a voice said, and I looked up into the face of a different version of me.

Like me (and Josephine), she had pale skin, unruly red

hair, and freckles. But her eyes were green, so vibrant that they seemed to shine. Her hands were held up, kind of defensively, and she was dressed like she'd stepped out of a medieval adventure novel: browns and greens, with high boots, leggings, and a plain tunic. Pouches and leather things I didn't recognize hung from a belt with intricate tooling on it. Her hair was short enough that I second-guessed her gender for a moment; plus she honestly had the kind of face that could have been male or female.

"Yes," Josephine said from behind me. "He is. I'm Josephine." I'm glad she was able to form sentences—I felt like I was going to pass out with the sudden influx of oxygen. I pressed the bandanna to my face again, wiping away the dust before tying it to my belt, forcing myself to breathe slowly.

"I'm Jari," she said, and the name tugged at my memory.

Now, don't get me wrong. I used to live on Base with roughly five hundred versions of me, all of whom had names that started with a *J* sound. Even if their names were in a different language, or a mathematical equation, it could generally be translated to a *J* sound. Saying that this girl's name tugged at my memory would have seemed vastly unimportant, except for one small thing: I'd never seen her before.

After a moment, I had it. "You're one of the twins," I said.

She nodded. "Yes. My brother is on his way."

"Twins?" Josephine asked. "We can be twins?"

"It's rare," I said. "In fact, it was unheard of—but, yes, we can be twins. Apparently." I smiled at Jari.

"It is not so uncommon to me," she said. "I find it more disturbing that there are so many of you who are not twins. I could not imagine being without my brother."

"Did it give you an advantage at InterWorld?" Josephine asked. "Like, in training?"

"We did not have much chance to find out," Jari said.

"I never even got to meet them," I explained. "They were brought onto the ship right before I left. They're from a high magic world. Remember, I explained about the arc of magic and science. . . ." I trailed off, looking at Jari again. Her hands weren't held up defensively, as I'd first thought. She was holding the dust and ash at bay, encasing us in a protective bubble of oxygen. I'd assumed (stupidly) that she'd had some sort of gadget on her at first, but she looked like she wouldn't even know the difference between a grav-disk and a cell phone.

"How are you doing that?" Josephine asked.

"My particular gift," she said. "Everyone on my world has one. I can adapt to any environment, or create one of my choosing in a small sphere around me. That is why they sent my brother and me out to gather food."

"He can do the same thing?" I asked.

"He can change himself," she explained, and turned to look up at the sky. Or, where I presumed the sky would be; there was nothing beyond our little sphere but a miasma of debris. "You do not think the appearance of a larger predator during your fight with the bird monster was coincidence, do you?" She smiled, abruptly lifting one arm to the sky—and an enormous red-tailed hawk came gliding out of the cloud of ash to rest upon her leather-covered forearm. He settled with a shuffling of wings, tilting his head at us.

"This is my brother, Jarl," she said, and the hawk gave a quiet chirp. "He is not usually so feathery," she added with a smile.

"Nice to meet you," Josephine said, and I could tell from her tone that she'd once again decided this was all absurd and she was just gonna go with it.

"Same here," I said, looking into the bird's eyes. Bright green, like Jari's.

"Jarl," Jari said, getting the bird's attention. They seemed to confer for a moment, just looking at each other, though the bird showed little or no reaction and neither of them spoke again.

Finally, she gave a bounce of her arm and the hawk spread his wings, launching himself into the air. He disappeared into the miasma and was gone.

"Are you and your brother—" I began.

"Telepathic?" she interrupted, then smiled. "In a sense. What we have is known as kinesthetic telepathy. When he found you earlier, he sent me an image of what he was seeing. When I caught up with you, I sent him a feeling of triumph, so he knew to join us."

"And you knew I was about to ask, because you sensed I was curious?"

"No." Her smiled widened. "We have been asked that several times since we met all of you. I assumed it would be your question, as well. I can utilize telepathy with my brother but no one else."

"Fair enough," I said, though something she'd said was nagging at me. "You were looking for us, specifically?"

"Yes. Joeb sent us out to find you."

I let out a quiet breath. Joeb was also a name I recognized. He was a senior officer on InterWorld, and someone I thought of as a friend. As far as I knew, he had been on InterWorld when the HEX ship had found it. He should be stuck in the warp field like everyone else. If he wasn't, and he had the twins with him . . . maybe there were more of us here than I thought.

Maybe we had more of a chance than I'd realized.

"How did he know we were here? Did he sense us Walk?"

"You will have to ask him," she said, and gestured for us to follow her.

"Who's Joeb?" Josephine asked as we walked through the thick red clouds, safe in our bubble of oxygen.

"Another one of us. A senior officer at InterWorld, from an Earth pretty close to ours. He's a lot like me, I guess. Older, maybe." Joeb was, in fact, a lot like me—but if I had to be honest, he was even more like Jay. He had a sort of big-brother aura to him, and tended to look after all the new recruits; that was probably how he'd wound up on this world with the twins. "He's a good guy," I said. He'd been one of the few people to start talking to me after I first came to InterWorld. We'd talked about family, since in his world, his youngest sibling was a girl instead of a boy, and her nickname was Mouse instead of Squid. There were always little similarities like that among all of us.

"He is," Jari agreed, navigating her way around the terrain. There were rocks here, sometimes, and gnarled little black things that might have once been trees. The only time I could see them was when the circle of clear air brushed past them, allowing us a glimpse of things here and there as we walked; otherwise they were faint shapes distorted by smoke. "He and four others came for us—my brother and me—on our world. There were other things, too, dangerous things we were running from."

"I know what that's like," Josephine said, shooting me a dark look.

"So do I," I reminded her, and Jari kept talking as we walked. I paced myself carefully; even though we hadn't gone far, I was already feeling a strain in my calves. And my shoulder, after all that activity—as we walked, I pulled a roll of bandages out of my backpack and tied them into a makeshift sling to take some of the weight off it.

"Yes, Joeb said they'd come to capture us when we first

realized our Walking power," Jari continued. "Jarl and I did not think we would have any other abilities beyond our gifts, but . . ." She trailed off, remembering.

"But then you figured out how to Walk," I guessed.

"Yes. It was amazing . . . at first. But then the bad ones came for us, and we ran. We made it back to our world, but they pursued us. That was when Joeb and the others came. They were all very brave, and took injuries helping us . . . but Joeb made sure to talk to us after we came back to the sky dome, and make certain we were all right. Then the Captain sent us out—"

"The Old Man did?" I interrupted. "Why?"

"Old Man," she repeated, sounding amused. "Joeb said that some people call him that."

"Most of us do, honestly. Why did he send you off? And when?"

"I do not know why," she said, looking briefly irritated at the interruptions. "You will have to ask Joeb."

"Where are we even going?" Josephine asked. "Is there any part of this world that isn't completely messed up, or does everyone just hold their breath all the time? Or do you have another ship?"

"We do not have a ship," she said, "but the dust only reaches so far."

It was at that moment that I realized the strain I was feeling in my legs wasn't because of how far we'd walked, it was because we were going uphill. I ignored the sudden thud of my heart against my chest. The thought of going anywhere near another mountain was daunting, at the least. . . .

I heard a hawk cry out above me, and looked up. Habit, really; I hadn't expected to see anything. To my surprise, though, I did. Barely visible, so faint I thought I'd imagined it, there was the soft glow of sunlight and the shadow of a bird passing over us. The miasma was thinning.

"It's a little farther," Jari said.

"So you and your brother can send each other emotions?"

"Yes, and we are often aware of the other's general location."

"Have you ever done it by accident?" Josephine asked.

"When we were younger, yes. Not as much now. If we are in pain or afraid, we often think of the other first, and then those emotions may send by mistake. Jarl once broke his arm playing by the foxwillow in the last summer days, and I knew immediately." There was something in her voice as she mentioned the incident, the casual way she spoke of things I'd never heard of reminding me of my own summers taking day trips to the beach with my family or when my sister and I ate Popsicles in the shade of the giant tree in our front yard. There was a sense of familiar fondness and a deep sense of loss; whatever a foxwillow was, Jari would probably never see one again. I would probably never see that giant oak tree again, either.

She glanced at me, and I offered a smile. Josephine was silent as she walked behind me. We both understood.

"This way," Jari said before I could say anything else, veering off to the right. The air was clean enough now that I could see the path outside our bubble, and we were definitely up in the mountains. The incline got sharper, and the air got gradually thinner.

"We aren't going to run out of oxygen or anything, are we?" Josephine asked.

"I doubt the mountain goes that high," I said, and she reached out to punch my arm. The good arm, thankfully.

"I know *that*. I meant the bubble we're in."

"Oh," I said, glancing around. That might actually be a legitimate concern.

"We are not in a bubble," Jari explained. "I am purifying the air around us in a small radius as we walk. You could easily reach outside of my range, if you wished."

"And you can do that anywhere? Even underwater?"

"Yes." She sounded proud. "Underwater, far underground, anywhere. It is specifically the ability to create the environment I need to survive, no matter what is around me."

"And you said you can adapt, too?" Josephine asked.

"Yes. I can either create the bubble for those I am with, or I can allow myself to breathe wherever I am."

"Do you grow gills or anything? Like, do you change your shape?"

"No, that is my brother's gift. He can become a water dweller; I can simply dwell in the water as is." She sounded irritated again; I was beginning to guess that she thought her brother's shape-shifting was a better ability than hers.

"That's really cool," Josephine said, and then we had to explain the colloquialism to Jari. By the time we got that sorted out, the air had cleared up enough that Jari dropped her not-bubble, and we walked into a makeshift base.

My knees went weak with relief. There were at least half a dozen temp camps, which could fit four people if you got cozy. There were twice that many Walkers doing various chores, and I recognized most of them—and one in particular, a girl most recognizable by her beautiful white wings.

"Jo!" I shouted, surprising myself as I darted forward. I was further surprised when she moved forward as well, meeting me in a hug.

Though Jo was one of the first people I'd interacted with at InterWorld, our relationship had always been chilly at best. Still, she was a teammate and (as far as I was concerned) a friend, and the first of either I'd seen in four or five days.

I hugged her tightly, though I was careful of her wings and she was careful of my shoulder. She pulled back almost immediately, looking embarrassed at her uncharacteristic exuberance. "Joey," she said, her voice heavy with relief. "You're—" She cut herself off from saying the word *okay*; I obviously wasn't all that okay, given the sling, wrist brace, and number of bandages on me.

"Alive," I filled in. "So are you. I'm glad," I said honestly, and we exchanged wry smiles. It was kind of like that right now; "alive" was about as good as we could hope for.

"I am also pleased to see you relatively well, though not uninjured," said another voice, one I would have recognized immediately even if not for the overabundance of formality in his tone.

"Hey, Jai!" Oh, what the hell—I hugged him, too, something he accepted with a hint of surprise. "Are you all right? I haven't seen you since . . ." I trailed off, not knowing what to call it. I couldn't say *the accident*, because it hadn't been one.

"I was fortunate enough to remain mostly unscathed," he said, "and I attempted to provide the same fate for our comrades. With little success," he added softly, his brown face filling with sorrow. I squeezed his shoulder.

"It would have been a lot worse without you," I said.

A small crowd was gathering around us, a crowd of people I recognized. They all took turns waving or greeting me, saying they were glad to see me or expressing relief that I was alive and here. There was the rest of my team aside from J/O: Josef, twice my size and built of thick, dense muscle, and Jakon, my sleek, furry wolflike cousin, and others who weren't on my team but had missed me anyway. J'r'ohoho, the centaur from a primitive world who'd nevertheless excelled in his science classes, and Jaya, with her red-gold hair and sweet voice.

They were all here, all glad to see me. It was a homecoming, of sorts, the kind I hadn't yet had at InterWorld. No one here had been glad to see me before, had given me hugs, or said they'd missed me. It was nice, not just for myself, but because Josephine was watching with a quiet understanding. I was glad she could see the camaraderie we felt for each other firsthand.

"How did you get here?" I asked finally, raising my voice to be heard above the chatter.

"That's something you and I should discuss," said a new voice, firm but not unkind, and a few people stepped aside to reveal Joeb.

"Hey," I said in greeting, another wave of relief washing through me. It wasn't just that I was glad to see him. He and Jai were both senior officers, which meant I wouldn't be the only one making decisions now. I didn't have to do this all on my own anymore.

"Come sit," he said, gesturing to a few travel cots that were set up around a portable heater. It was warmer now that we could actually feel the sunlight, but I imagined it got cold up here.

Joeb and I sat down on a cot. All the others followed, some also sitting on cots and others on the ground, leaning against one another and otherwise getting comfortable. Apparently, it was story time.

"The Old Man pulled me into his office six days ago," Joeb began, his brown eyes serious. "He said there had been a security breach, a leak he'd just discovered."

"It was Joaquim," I said. A murmur went through those listening.

"It can't have been," someone said.

"We'd've known," someone else insisted, and a few other voices rose up in agreement.

"It *was* Joaquim," Joeb said clearly, his voice rising once again above the chatter. He let that sink in for a moment, glancing out over the faces of those assembled. "Captain Harker confirmed it before we left."

I looked out at them, too, seeing the same disbelief I had felt, the same betrayal that had been twisting at me for days. "He's dead," I said, and Joeb looked at me. "He was a creation of Binary . . . and HEX," I said, and another murmur went through the crowd. "They're working together now. They used a combination of science and magic to create what they call FrostNight, and they used me and Joaquim to power it. Acacia helped me escape, but Joaquim was . . ."

"Killed?" asked Jo, when I faltered.

"Used up," I said, unable to look at her. I couldn't look at anyone; I kept remembering Joaquim's face, still contorted into a mask of fear and anger, no emotion or depth or life left in his eyes at all. "He was powered by magic. And us, of the essences that are stolen when we're caught by HEX."

Now I did look at her, and all of them, my gaze roaming over the faces of these comrades who were just like me. They all looked as sick as I felt.

"FrostNight," Joeb said, after a moment of silence. "What is it?"

I took a breath. "Basically? A self-perpetuating supercontinuum that rearranges all of time and space in its path."

A short silence followed my statement. Those who'd had any manner of basic classes at InterWorld Prime looked appropriately concerned. Others, such as Jari and Josephine, looked like they had absolutely no clue what the hell I'd just said.

"Okay," said Joeb, who was one of the ones looking concerned. "What is its path, exactly?"

"Everywhere. It's a self-aware manifold; it can reach into any dimension."

"It has to disperse eventually," someone ventured from the crowd. "Doesn't it?"

"I don't *know*," I snapped, then put a hand to my forehead. I hadn't meant to be short, I was just frustrated; I didn't know nearly as much about this as I needed to. I'd seen it created, but I still knew next to nothing. "It was powered by *us*, by me and Joaquim and all the souls they'd infused him with. They got all of . . . them, all of him, but I escaped."

"How?" someone else asked, and I wasn't sure if I was imagining the hint of suspicion or not.

"Acacia," I said, and Joeb held up a hand.

"Hold on," he said, looking at me sympathetically. "Why don't I tell you our side of the story, and then you can fill in the gaps for us."

I nodded, grateful, and he continued. "The Old Man called me into his office two days after we extracted the twins." He nodded to Jari and the hawk. "He said there was a leak in InterWorld, and that everyone was in danger. He instructed me and several other officers to take small groups of people off Base for training, and not to return until we heard from him. He also gave me an ADT"—he pulled an advanced dimensional tracker, a small, circular device, from his pocket—"and told me to keep an eye out for you."

"For me?" I accepted the tracker as he handed it to me, staring down the screen. It had exactly one blip, a little red dot in the center. Me. "I'll be damned," I muttered, staring at the dot. I remembered sitting in the stark white infirmary, barely feeling the shot as it stabbed into my arm, still numb from my injuries and Jerzy's funeral the day before. "He had me injected with a tracer the same day he sent you off Base. Hours before, I'll bet. He said it was for my own safety, but now I'm not so sure." After all, this wasn't the first time the tracer had come in handy. The Old Man had to have known it would, but how?

Acacia, I realized, my hand clenching around the ADT. She was a Time Agent. She must have known this was going to happen, must have warned the Old Man.

I did my best to fight down a surge of anger, and instead handed the ADT back to Joeb and tried to concentrate on what he was saying. Why couldn't she have warned him about any of the other horrible things that had happened in the last week? Jerzy's death? Binary and HEX working together? The Professor sacrificing his "son" to create a self-aware soliton that will erase everything in the Multiverse, for God's sake! She didn't find any of that to be *half* as important as having me injected with a tracer?

"Joey?" Joeb's voice pulled me out of my thoughts, and I realized I'd completely lost track of the conversation.

"Sorry. What?"

"I asked if you knew why Captain Harker hadn't contacted us yet. I mean, I assumed I was waiting for you, but I imagine you haven't brought us orders to go back to base."

I shook my head. "No. They're . . . InterWorld is compromised," I said, hating the words as they left my lips. There was the sound of a collective intake of breath from everyone sitting around me. "It's been locked on to by a HEX ship. They're running, I don't know where to and I don't know for how long. I think they're stuck in a perpetual temporal warp, at least for now."

"I was afraid of that," Joeb said. At my look, he shrugged. "The InterWorld formula is . . . it feels like a broken link right now. Like it wouldn't take me anywhere if I tried to use it."

He sighed, reaching up to rub the back of his neck, turning his head this way and that to stretch muscles made tense by worry and stress. I knew the feeling. "So that's my side of it. We've been sitting on this mountain for the better part of a week now, running some rudimentary training and waiting to either hear from the Old Man or see your little dot show up on the ADT."

"What about the other officers with their teams? Do you know where they are?"

"I don't know if any of them actually made it off Base," he admitted. "I grabbed my recruits pretty quickly—my teams, and what I could of yours." He nodded to where Jo, Jakon, Josef, and Jai were sitting nearby, listening.

"Most of mine were injured in the rockslide," I murmured, more or less to myself. Why had the Old Man had him take the injured Walkers off Base?

Joeb grinned at me. I blinked at the expression; for obvious reasons, his smile seemed kind of out of place. "They wouldn't take no for an answer when they found out we were going off Base," he explained. Jakon bared her teeth at me in her signature fierce smile, and Josef shot me a thumbs-up.

I hung my head, giving a quiet laugh. That was my team, all right.

"Okay," I said, the word coming out as a sigh. "Ready to hear my side of it?"

It didn't take me long to tell Joeb and the others everything that had happened to me. I had told it so many times, to Mr. Dimas and to Josephine, that I did so mechanically now, letting my brain detach from what I was saying and think about other things. Like how to get them all back to InterWorld Beta.

I hadn't expected to run into so many Walkers at once. Honestly, I was concerned that having so many of them here would draw unwanted attention from our enemies, especially if we tried to Walk. Walking, if you weren't careful about it, tended to alert the capture agents of either HEX or Binary. Not always, but they did have specific sensors for it. That's how they'd find us, when we first discovered our power, before we even knew what was happening. . . .

Would Hue be able to take all of us at once? Or, if he was covering me, would *I* be able to Walk all of us through time? Though that many of us Walking at once would still have to blip some sensors, somewhere.

But, assuming FrostNight had been released, would they even care about what we were doing? *You will not be able to Walk far enough away,* Lord Dogknife had gloated to me. He'd left me alive on my home world; he obviously wasn't too concerned with what I would or wouldn't do. Would they even be paying attention enough to notice if that many of us Walked at once?

Damn it. There was too much I didn't know.

"So, when Acacia sent me into the future to keep me safe," I continued, "she sent me to a future version of Inter-World. I was able to get back, thanks to the tracer the Old Man injected me with, and Hue. Hue can act like an encounter suit and form himself to me. When he does, I can Walk to any timeline. It's like . . . like I become multidimensional myself."

"Is it safe?" someone asked.

"Yes." Surprisingly, it was Josephine who spoke up. "Don't get me wrong, I'm still not sure I trust that little balloon, but we Walked through time easily enough. And we found you."

I nodded. "So, we do have a ship. It's just a matter of getting to it, and powering it once we're there. Once we get the warp engines up and running, we can take the ship to our own timeline."

"Then what?" Joeb asked, watching me carefully.

I took a breath. "Then we split into two groups. One group is responsible for extracting new Walkers, and the other will be training. Hard."

"Okay," Joeb said, holding up a hand. "I know why we're getting new Walkers; it's what we've always done, and it ensures HEX and Binary won't find them first. But what, specifically, are we training for?"

"To stop FrostNight."

A moment of silence followed, then Joeb asked, "How?"

"I don't know. But, if we can get InterWorld Beta up and

running, we can use the library to research possible solutions." That was met with more silence, and I sighed. "I know it's not much of a plan. If any of you can think of anything better, believe me, I am all ears."

"How long do we have?" Joeb said, after the silence had stretched for a moment more.

"I don't know. It's been days since I was dropped on my world. We have to act now. It may already be too late, but it's either we do anything and everything we can, or we roll over and give up."

"No one's suggesting we do nothing," Jo spoke up, a little sharply. I took a breath—I'd been starting to get frustrated, and Jo's tone was a warning, a reminder that getting upset wouldn't fix anything.

"I know," I said, glancing briefly at her in thanks. "And I know you're all willing to do whatever is needed."

"One thing at a time," Joeb said. "The first thing we have to figure out is how to get back Joey's InterWorld."

"InterWorld Beta," I corrected under my breath. I wasn't comfortable with it being referred to as *mine*.

"How many of us do you think your mudluff could take at once?"

"I don't know. He took me with no problem, and he managed to take me and Josephine, but I don't know if he could take all of us. I don't know what would happen if we tried and something went wrong."

"Better safe than sorry," Joeb said.

"We're not being safe either way," Jo pointed out, "with so many of us here. If what Joey said about Joaquim and the way they powered him is right, they might be able to do that again. They might able to sense us, the way we can sense each other. They might come here."

"Would they bother?" Joeb asked, echoing my earlier thoughts.

"I don't know," I said again. It felt like the millionth time I'd said those words in the last few minutes, and it was infuriating. I wasn't being any help to anyone. "Lord Dogknife seemed pretty confident that there wouldn't be anything I could do to stop them. Whether they'll be watching us anyway or not, I . . ." I trailed off, unwilling to say those three words again. "I can't say," I said instead. It was a little better.

"Better safe than sorry," Joeb repeated. "Let's assume they can—and will—sense us, whether we stay in a group or Walk. That means we have to get as many of us to Inter-World Beta as we can. They won't be able to follow us there, right?"

"Right," I said, hoping desperately that I *was* right. I had to be. They didn't have any way to travel through time, not like I could if I had Hue with me. "They can't Walk through time."

"No one can, except your mudluff. Thankfully." Joeb smiled at me.

And Acacia, I thought unwillingly, and managed a smile back. I wondered if what Acacia did was technically Walking, or something entirely different. We hadn't had much time to discuss the mechanics of it.

"So, since we don't know what would happen if something went wrong while we tried to Walk through time, we should go in small groups," Joeb stated. "But, since we have to assume they'll be able to sense us Walk and might send out scouts, we should take as many at once as possible. Thoughts?"

"I think the best compromise is to go in two groups," I ventured. "Split right down the middle, and do it that way. Agreed?"

I glanced around. Most of the Walkers looked doubtful, but some of them were nodding. It really did seem like the best option.

"Okay," I said. "I want Josephine to take both groups. She's the quietest Walker I've ever met; if she takes you, you'll definitely get there undetected. We'll send any of the injured first—"

"Which should include you," Joeb said. I shook my head.

"Not a chance."

"You're pretty beat up," Jo pointed out.

"I'm not going first," I said. "I'm making sure you all get there safely, and that's final."

"You're the only one who knows firsthand about

everything that's going on," Jo insisted. "If we lose you, we're stumbling around in the dark."

"We're doing that anyway. You know as much as I do now. Jo," I continued, when she started to argue again, "I want you in charge of the first group."

As I'd hoped, that surprised her enough to derail her next protest. Instead, she said "Me? Joeb is . . ."

"I'll stay with the second group," Joeb said.

Jo frowned. "But Jai's a senior officer, too."

"And he needs a translator," I told her, and there was a quiet ripple of laughter. Jai smiled serenely, not minding the joke at his expense.

"Any and all wounded—except me," I clarified, as Jo started to shoot me a glare, "will go with the first group. This includes Jakon, Josef, Jai, Jo, and Josephine. Jo is team lead. Then Josephine will come back here, and take the second group. Agreed?"

"I am predominantly uninjured," Jai finally pointed out.

"But you're also a senior officer, and I want you there to help Jo in case something goes wrong," I told him.

"Very sensible," he agreed. "Shall we apportion ourselves into commensurate assemblages?"

I looked at Jo.

"Yes, let's split into two even groups," she said, catching my look. She almost smiled as she spoke.

I sat down with Jo, Jai, Josephine, and Joeb to figure out how we should be divided, while everyone else broke camp. Neither task took long, as five of us were already put in one group, and there hadn't been much of a camp to begin with.

All told, there were roughly fifteen of us in each group (specifically, there were fourteen in my group and fifteen in the other—we always made a point to do an exact count for any mission). We stood a ways apart from each other, in case anything went wrong. Josephine looked stoic and determined, though I was sure she had to be nervous. I smiled at her as we stepped forward.

"Okay, Hue," I said, and the little mudluff floated up from where he'd been in the hood of my sweatshirt. It was weird; while I rarely ever saw him shrink or grow, he always seemed to fit wherever he needed to. He was now bigger than the hood he'd been resting in, about the balloon size he usually was. I hadn't even noticed him there, so he must have made himself smaller. I supposed that was one benefit of being multidimensional.

"C'mere, Hue," Josephine called. He floated over, settling on her outstretched hand. I was worried that he wasn't going to cooperate with her, or would bond with her for long enough to let her get back to InterWorld Beta and then wander off. I was hoping, if that did happen, that he would come back to me; the last thing we needed was to be stranded here until Hue decided to meander back. The little guy hadn't let me down yet, though. He'd wandered off for weeks at a time, but he'd always come back.

"Do what you did with us before," I urged, when Hue perched on Josephine's hand. He flickered from blue to white, then flashed silver for a second. "Yeah, like that. Help her get back to the ship." I wasn't sure why silver reminded me of the way he'd flowed over me, but it did. . . . After a moment, though, I had it. The silver encounter suit I'd worn once had flowed over me in the same way. Hue had a very specific way of communicating with me, mostly seeming to rely on my visual memory. I'd always sort of wondered about that.

Hue bobbed up and down a few times, seeming to bounce against Josephine's hand. Then he moved sideways, except part of him stayed on the tips of her fingers. He started to move around her like that, covering her slowly, like he had before. I suddenly felt anxious, like the first time my mom had let my little sister walk to the corner store by herself. I'd been certain she'd inherited my horrible sense of direction and would get hopelessly lost on the way there.

"Remember to center yourself," I told her. "You're not making a path, you're—"

"Finding one that's already there," she said, standing still as Hue spread to her feet and up her torso. "I know. I've Walked several times over the past few days, remember?"

"Okay, okay. As for the rest of you"—I tilted my head to address the dozen or so Walkers behind her—"Josephine is

Walking, you're following. Don't lose her. You won't be able to find the path on your own; you can't see the ones that weave through time." I wondered if Acacia saw things the same way we did; if the timestream was like a bunch of paths that she could follow forward or backward.

"You guys ready?" Josephine asked, and was rewarded with silence; we were all trained well enough to know that if there was a chorus of yeses, we wouldn't hear the one person who was saying no. She glanced at me and I nodded, so she took Jo's hand and inhaled—

—and vanished, which was what it looked like when someone Walked. They were gone in the blink of an eye, like they'd disappeared into thin air, midstep. I could feel them leave, because of my own ability to Walk; it was like sensing a door opening and closing when you're alone in a room. You know it happened, even if you weren't looking.

"Okay," I said, turning to my group. There were a few faces I recognized; Joeb, of course, and the twins, who had asked to stay with him. Jarl was no longer a bird, and his resemblance to his sister was striking. The one hope I had of telling them apart was the neatly trimmed beard on his face; his hair was just as short as Jari's and he had her same red hair and bright green eyes.

I put a few more names to faces, like Jirho and Jijoo, and one or two others I saw around the back. They were all people I was used to seeing here and there, but there weren't many of them (aside from J'r'ohoho) I had regular classes or training sessions with. "It shouldn't take more than a few minutes for Josephine to get back." *Assuming everything goes according to plan, please oh* please, *just this once let everything go according to plan. . . .* "So we'd better get ready."

"If she's traveling through time," Jirho piped up from the front of the group, "shouldn't she be able to come back immediately? Just a few seconds after she left?"

"It doesn't work that way," I said. Conversations with a Time Agent had given me a basic grasp of this stuff, and I hoped I sounded sure enough that they wouldn't question me. "She's still anchored to her personal timeline. She can stay in the past for as long as she likes, but time will keep moving. If she stays for five minutes, she'll return five minutes from when she left."

"That's disappointing," someone else said. "What's the point in time traveling if you can't go back to fix mistakes?"

"What's the point of being able to Walk?" I shot back, and a few of them looked thoughtful. There was no point, really. It was just something we could do, and we were lucky enough (or unlucky enough, depending on your perspective) to be able to use it to our advantage in a war.

"Once we get to InterWorld Beta," I moved on, "there will still be a lot to do. I've got the basic functions running on solar power for now, but we still have to charge the transducers. Once we get the soliton array working, the engines will be able to move us forward and backward again. Then we can get the ship back to *our* timeline, and we won't have to rely on Hue to get us back to base."

"How are we powering the transducers?" J'r'ohoho asked. It always amused me to hear the centaur version of me talk about technology; though he'd come from a tribal society that had practically just invented the wheel, he'd taken very quickly to all his science lessons and was usually top of the class.

It was so like him to ask the hard questions.

"We'll find a way when we get there," Joeb cut in, probably sensing that my answer was about to be another version of *I don't know*. I was, again, immensely grateful. "Let's worry about one thing at a time."

I had only just finished speaking when I once more had the sense of a door opening nearby, which fortunately meant we had one *less* thing to worry about. Josephine stepped back through thin air a few feet from where she'd been previously, looking quite pleased with herself. Hue (again seeming smaller than he should be) was perched on her shoulder.

"Welcome back," I said, over the small round of cheering that bubbled up as she reappeared. "Everything go okay?"

"No problems," she said. "I dropped them off in the courtyard." She paused, her pride at a job well done fading. "Some of them were pretty upset to see it like that."

I nodded, glancing at the others. I had explained about

how I'd been sent to future InterWorld and found it destroyed, but knowing it wasn't the same as seeing it. InterWorld Base Town was home as much as the places we'd all come from had been, and seeing it like that was more than hard. It was hopeless. It felt like we'd already lost. "We'll get it fixed up again," I told her, though I was saying it for everyone. "It'll be better than new, and then we'll get back to *our* InterWorld and rescue the rest of us. It'll feel like home again."

I held out both hands, one to Josephine and one to Joeb, and nodded at the former. "Let's go. Why don't you do the honors?"

"Oh? I figured you'd want to do it yourself, you're such a mother hen," she shot at me, but she looked pleased. "Okay, Hue. One more time."

Hue (who seemed to be a shade or two paler than his usual neutral color; this probably *was* tiring him out) flowed over her once again, barely brushing over my fingers where Josephine was carefully holding my injured hand. Then she Walked, and so did Joeb, myself, the twins, and the nine others with us.

It felt different this time. It was like stepping through a door, as usual, but we found nothing on the other side. No path. Darkness closed around us as we went over the threshold, so quickly that none of us had time to warn one another. I felt Josephine stumble and fall, and I followed her, pitching headlong into a void.

Joeb's hand slipped from mine, and my mouth opened and my vocal cords vibrated with a shout, but there was no sound. There was nothing at all.

I clutched tight to Josephine's hand, but I wasn't even sure I could still feel it in mine. I thought I smelled perfume, something sweet, like roses. I heard something, too, an echo that might have been a breathy laugh, and then the darkness swallowed me whole.

CHAPTER SIX

IT'S NOT THAT I passed out, exactly. When you pass out (which, as I'm sure you know, I've done a few times in my life), there's a sort of white-hot feeling around your forehead when you regain consciousness. Waking up isn't even the right term for it. It's like coming back to yourself after you've been gone, except you're not really sure where you've been.

That's what it felt like at first, but I knew I hadn't actually passed out because I didn't have that white-hot headache. It was more like when you walk into a room for a specific reason, but then can't remember why, so you just stand there and feel lost.

I opened my eyes to complete and total blackness, and my first thought was *Why did I come here?* Then I remembered Josephine, and trying to Walk through time, and my second thought was *Where is everyone?*

I was starting to see things in my field of vision that

made me worry I *was* about to pass out, little bright motes of light that were there and gone when I tried to look at them. They swirled and wove around me dizzyingly, so I stopped trying to focus on them. There was a weird feeling in the air and that sweet smell that reminded me of spring and the color pink.

I had to find my friends. I didn't even care where *I* was, as long as I found Josephine and everyone else.

I tried to sit up and realized that I had nothing to brace myself against. I was floating, weightless, suspended in mid-air. The white lights dancing around me were stars, or at least they looked like stars. I'd never been sure, but seeing them cemented my reality. I knew where I was.

This was the Nowhere-at-All.

I'd been here before, twice. I'd hoped to never come back. It was kind of like the In-Between, except where the In-Between was *everything,* the Nowhere-at-All was nothing. It was entirely dark, not dark like you couldn't see anything but more like there was nothing but dark *to* see. There was nothing here, aside from little lights that may have been far-off stars or tiny, close sparks, and yet you always felt like you weren't alone.

It was HEX's domain.

I couldn't move my arms or my legs. I shoved down a surge of panic and lifted my head to look around. My wrists and ankles were restrained by an invisible force, and I realized that some of the little white lights I'd thought were big and far away were actually close and very small. They were spread out around me in a pattern that I first mistook for an unfamiliar constellation. It was symmetrical and, honestly, beautiful, arcing out above and below me to either side. Horizontal lines looped back and forth over diagonal ones pulled taut, strings of tiny white sparks like you'd see around a Christmas tree or like morning dew on a spiderweb.

A spiderweb . . .

I still couldn't move my arms and legs. Adrenaline surged through me (I was calling it that, but with the realization that I was trapped in a giant spiderweb, it was probably just panic), and I wiggled with all my might, but I couldn't see anything but those little white lights that might have been stars.

"*Josephine!*" I yelled and heard my voice echo back to me. "*Joeb!*"

"I'm here," Joeb's voice called from somewhere to the left of me. I couldn't see him.

"Joeb!" a female voice called, also from the left, though it sounded farther away. "Jarl and I are here!"

"Most of us are, I think," Joeb said. "Everyone, sound off. One!"

"Two!" someone else's voice called, then it was "three," then, after a slight pause, "four!"

The interesting thing about a group of people—any

people, from any world—is that they often develop a sense of cohesion, a flow, a pattern. Back on my world, they'd done numerous studies on the flow of pedestrian traffic in big, densely populated cities like New York. The way people wove through crowds and around sidewalks while looking down at their cell phones is miraculous, and has something to do with social instinct. It's the thing that's *not* working when you run into someone in a hallway and then do a little dance trying to get around them.

It's also the same instinct that lets a roomful of people have a conversation; you develop a sense for when it's your turn to speak, or when someone else is going to. Like I said, some people are better at it than others. But we were all different versions of one another, which meant we had roughly the same instincts and social patterns.

"Five!" came a distant call from behind me, then "six" and "seven" in voices that sounded the same—probably the twins.

"Eight!" rang out to my right, and then I felt like it was my turn. "Nine!" I called, and the numbers went on. Sure, once or twice two people would start to say the same number, but one of them would always stop and go directly after. When no more voices rang out, we were at thirteen. We were missing one.

And I hadn't heard Josephine.

"We're missing one," Joeb called.

"It's Josephine," I said, and then someone screamed.

It was a startled sound, involuntary, loud and shrill. I knew it was one of us.

It came from behind me, and I craned my neck to the point of pain. I couldn't see anything but blackness and more stars. My heart pounded against my chest. I held my breath, racking my mind for something, anything to do or say.

"Jenna!" another voice from behind me yelled. "What's wrong?" There were two different girls named Jenna on base; the middle-Arc Greenvilles like the one I'd come from were more common than the fringe ones, so some of us had the same names. I knew both of them in passing; one had shared my Alchemical History class, and reminded me of my little sister. The other was a new recruit, shy and sweet, and I don't think she'd ever been out on a mission before. I thought I'd remembered seeing her in the crowd when we were preparing to leave, but I wasn't sure now. My mind had been elsewhere.

"Jirho, can you see her?" one of us shrilled, and I recognized in the voice the same panic that was threatening to bubble up inside me. I struggled against the light web, only succeeding in causing myself pain as I twisted my shoulder and wrist.

"No, I can't see anyone!" Both voices came from behind me. No one, yet, had called out from above or below me. It was like we were suspended in a line, or several lines.

Jenna screamed again, a long, thin sound that trailed off

into a wail and ended in a sputtering choke. It sounded . . . final.

"Everyone stay calm," Joeb called from my left, though I could hear the undercurrent of tension in his voice. "Focus and try to—"

"Demon spawn!" a thick, rich voice yelled. The gravely tenor was unmistakable; it held a slightly higher note in its fear, like a horse's neigh. J'r'ohoho. "You will not take— *eeeeaaaaggghhh!*"

Another scream cut through the blackness. The little white stars around me blurred as my eyes watered, but I was too stunned to cry. How could this be happening? *What* was happening?

The part of my mind that wasn't frozen in shock somehow made my mouth work. I ignored the gibbering voice in my head that was screaming *Don't draw its attention or you'll be next you idiot oh lord ohgodohgod*, and managed to put some amount of authority into my words. "Show yourself, coward! Or do you only stalk the helpless?" Archaic and dramatic, I know, but J'r'ohoho's last words were ringing in my mind. He'd always had a formality to his tone, and I'd always enjoyed hearing him talk science with his somewhat medieval speech.

I desperately hoped I'd get to hear it again.

We waited in horrible, horrible silence for an eternity that spanned a few seconds. It was horrible because I expected to hear another one of us die—*please oh please don't let them have died*—any moment, *any moment*, and the mix of waiting and praying made me feel sick.

"Little Harker," a voice said. It was a woman's voice, sweet and honeyed and revolting. I sagged with relief, letting out the breath I didn't know I'd been holding. I'd gotten its attention, whatever "it" was. That meant, for a moment at least, it wouldn't be hurting anyone else.

"Sweet little Harker," the voice said again, and something brushed flower-petal light against my cheek. There was a tingle of magic in the air. "I've been waiting so long."

I listened, but the voice fell silent. The sense of magic faded.

And someone else screamed, to my left.

"Waiting for what?" I screamed as well, before the other sound had even died. The words ripped themselves from my throat. *"What were you waiting for?"* I had to keep talking. I had to keep her attention.

"To thank you, little butterfly," she whispered. At least, it had the quality of a whisper, but it was loud and it echoed in the stillness. I could hear someone crying to my right, soft sobs that rubbed my nerves raw.

"For *what*?" The question came out like a growl. It may have made me sound fierce; it was actually just me trying to get words out through a throat made tight with the threat of tears.

"For showing me to my cocoon, wildfire," she said. I was confused at first, but then I realized the way she'd said that last word sounded like something she was calling me, like a nickname. "And for bringing all these little candles to feed me."

"Who are you?" I demanded, though I already had a nagging suspicion. It was more that I was terrified of losing her attention. I had to keep her talking.

"Mother Moth," she said, and some of the maybe stars in front of me started to fade. It was only some of them, though, and I squinted—and realized it wasn't that they were fading, it was that something was materializing in front of them. "Though that is not the name you knew me as."

"Lady Indigo," I whispered, as she appeared fully in front of me.

Now, I'd been prepared for something terrifying. I was trapped in something like a spiderweb, and the awful sounds I'd just heard had conjured images in my mind of monsters beyond comparison, anything from giant demons to Lord Dogknife himself.

I wasn't prepared for this.

When I'd first met Lady Indigo, before I'd ever come to InterWorld, she'd been human. Beautiful, in fact, with long dark hair and emerald-green eyes. She still had the eyes, starkly prominent in the hollow gauntness of her face. Her skin wasn't any kind of normal human flesh color now, not pinkish or tan or brown or black. It was red, crimson specifically, and see-through. I could see her skeleton beneath it, though that was all. There were no muscles, no organs.

I could see other bones as well, ones that didn't belong in a human. The most prominent were the ones that arched upward from her back, like . . . well, they looked a little like wings and a little like spider legs. There were eight of them in all, four on either side. They were huge, and stretched between them was webbing that looked to be fused together from the skins of a dozen different creatures. I recognized some of them from my zoology and paleozoology classes at InterWorld. Some of them probably hadn't ever been cataloged because no one who'd seen them could have possibly lived long enough to give them any other name than *oh lord, it's gonna eat me.*

The effect was sort of like an angry moth that was also a spider and a person, except it was a lot scarier than that. Especially combined with the look she was giving me. It was a sick sort of attraction, like I was the flame to her moth, prey to her spider, and a mate to her human, all at once. Like she wanted to nest in my skin.

I was shivering as she moved closer, the scent of death and roses overpowering me. "You . . . what happened to you?"

The last time I'd seen Lady Indigo had been two years ago, when my team and I were escaping from the HEX ship *Malefic.* I'd had a pouch of some kind of powder I'd picked up from the rendering room, that awful place where Walkers were dropped still alive into a cauldron and boiled down to their essence. I'd grabbed it in desperation, thrown it at her, and she'd been enveloped in red mist. I hadn't ever found out what happened to her.

I wished that was still the case.

"You stole my flesh," she whispered, one of those bone spider-leg wings reaching out to stroke my hair. "You reduced me to nothing, little Harker, nothing but magic and desire. But I survived, oh yes, I did. You are never truly alone in the Nowhere-at-All, and I proved stronger than any of them. I feasted, I did, and I learned. I learned . . ."

Her voice trailed off as something else caught her attention, something to the right of me. It was hard to tell on her transparent, red skin, but there might have been blood on her mouth. I wasn't sure.

Her eyes narrowed, and she shifted as though to move. "What did you learn?" I asked quickly, catching her attention again.

She looked back down at me, her face less than a foot away from mine and those spider-leg wings stretching out and over us both. "I learned how to feel your fire, little Walkersssss. . . ." She trailed off into a hiss, twitching once or twice, and suddenly turned her head to the side. She popped some of the vertebrae in her neck with a sound like cracking knuckles, one that set my teeth on edge. "And how," she continued, "to sssssssuck it all up . . ."

She smiled at me, a perfect, beautiful, human smile, except for the fact that I could see through her face. "Flames," she muttered. "Such beautiful flames. Beautiful butterflies. Mother Moth has all she needs, now."

It became obvious right then, as it really should have been before, that she was completely mad. Whatever had happened to her—if I'd gotten the powder from the rendering room, had it been part of the process used to boil us down to our essences? Is that what I'd somehow done?—it had clearly stolen her sanity. Although, that could have been attributed solely to being trapped in the Nowhere-at-All for a few years. . . .

"What do you mean, all you need?" I asked, but she wasn't looking at me anymore. "Indigo!" I shouted, and that got her attention.

She moved suddenly, all the points of her bone wing-legs digging into my sides. She was on top of me, hovering over me, and I could feel our skin touching. Hers felt slick and rubbery, and I tried to shrink back, but there was nowhere to go.

"You will address me as *Lady*," she hissed, right in my face. "I remember a time when you would have done anything I asked, little Harker, and I can make that time come again."

"Try it," I spat, though in truth I was terrified of her enchanting me again. The last time she'd cast a spell on me,

I would have walked happily off a cliff if she'd asked me to. I couldn't bear the thought of being under that kind of control again, but I wasn't about to let *her* know that.

"And so I shall, wildfire," she murmured, her lips close to my ear. "I'm going to eat all your friends and then make you *love me for it*."

I opened my mouth, but all that came out was a shocked, strangled sound. I was furious, and terrified. I had to do something. There *had* to be something I could do, but I couldn't Walk and I had no equipment on me, nothing to help me out of this web thing.

"I'll go with you," I said desperately. "Take me wherever you want, just—"

"Let them go? Such a noble Harker," she said, pushing against me and the web. She floated backward, the bone legs that had been digging into my sides arcing up behind her, looking more like wings again. "A valiant hero, defeating the evil sorceress, leaving her to wither and fester in the dark . . . Which little light should I drink from first?"

She was hovering about three feet from me now, impressive and terrible as she lifted a hand to point at me. "Duck," she said, and I was further confused. Then she smiled, pointing to my left. "Duck . . ."

She moved her hand farther, pointing at someone else I couldn't see. She stayed in front of me, so I could see her expression as she chose who was to die next. "Duck . . ."

Then, with no warning whatsoever, I couldn't quite see her anymore. Someone was blocking my view, their back to me, but I recognized the ratty backpack she wore. Josephine. She was suddenly *there*, between me and Lady Indigo, and then I heard a loud *crack* as she fired her .45.

Now, InterWorld didn't tend to use standard guns for two reasons. Mostly because we had access to things far more advanced, like plasma blasters. The other reason was most agents of Binary and HEX either were immune to pesky things like bullets or had ways of getting around them, like skin shields or magic. I wouldn't have expected a standard gun to do much damage to something that looked like *that*.

A short, startled scream ripped through the air, but this time it was Lady Indigo. Bullets, it seemed, would work.

Crack. The gun fired again, and Lady Indigo recoiled. Then another figure appeared, in a shimmer of violet light that made my heart leap into my throat. "Acacia!" I yelled, and then I got a haphazard impression of familiar violet eyes set in an unfamiliar face, and a glare that would wither stone. It wasn't Acacia. It was a boy about my age, wielding a katana-style sword that sported a blade of something other than steel, maybe jade. He raised the weapon over his head, facing me, and I had another instant to realize it was patterned gold and green, like a circuit board. Like Acacia's fingernails.

Then he struck, slicing the circuitry blade down toward

me. Despite the fact that this seemed like a rescue, I couldn't help a surge of adrenaline as he brought the weapon down. He was cutting it *close*—

I felt a sudden sting against my ear, but the web fell away behind me. I grabbed at the remaining bits of it, remembering that the Nowhere-at-All had its own gravity, and I could fall if I wasn't careful.

This new person who wasn't Acacia didn't seem to be having that problem; he cut me free of the web, then sped away toward the other ones. It was like he was gliding on nothing, skating on air. I remembered Acacia doing the same thing once, in the In-Between.

Crack. Josephine was still firing. I turned to look; she seemed to be standing on nothing, Hue hovering next to her. A second later I realized she was standing on a grav-board. I had no idea where she might have gotten it, or where she'd been for the past few minutes, not that it was important right now; she was still shooting, and I'd counted at least three shots. Those plus the one she'd fired at Hue meant she was at least halfway to empty on a standard .45, and Lady Indigo was still moving.

"Joey!" Joeb was free now, too, also clinging to his web. I turned to face him, seeing what was behind me for the first time. I'd been right in my estimation; we'd been suspended in separate webs, in a giant circle, facing outward.

"Get everyone out of here!" I yelled. "Walk!"

"Where?" he shouted back, as two more shots rang out and Lady Indigo let out a high-pitched sound that was half wail, half hiss.

"Anywhere, just Walk! I'll find—"

"Stay," the boy with the circuitry sword commanded, his voice carrying easily over the commotion. "I'll take you!" He was gathering up the threads of white light that had made up the spiderwebs, somehow weaving them together and drawing us all inward. I hadn't noticed it until now, but I was moving. The spiderweb I was clutching was being drawn into the center, with all the others. I was moving farther away from Josephine and Lady Indigo.

Click went Josephine's .45, and she shoved it back into her makeshift holster as Lady Indigo lunged for her. One of Lady Indigo's skeletal wings drooped slightly to one side, though she was still flying; she swooped down toward Josephine, who kicked off with her grav-board, the two beginning a grotesque aerial dance as Lady Indigo attacked and Josephine dodged. I hadn't had any disks to train her with back at Inter-World Beta, but she seemed to have gotten the hang of it. I recalled the older kid next door when I was growing up; he'd given me some skateboard training before I'd skinned both elbows and lost interest. Maybe Josephine had been better at it than I had. She certainly looked like she knew what she was doing, weaving in and out of the webs still hanging in the air and expertly avoiding Lady Indigo's attacks. They were spiraling higher and higher, farther from the webs as the mysterious newcomer drew us all closer together.

Josephine zipped closer to me, banking a hard left on the grav-board and moving back the way she'd come. Hue was still hovering around her, alternating various colors of distress. Lady Indigo whipped out a wing, the bone striking Josephine directly in the torso. She doubled over, the grav-board flying out from under her as she started to fall back down toward us.

"Hue!" I yelled. "Get the disk!"

My little mudluff friend didn't even hesitate. He sped toward the grav-board, not slowing as he approached it, and completely enveloped it in his body. Then he vanished, reappearing next to me faster than I could even blink. Above us, Lady Indigo was wheeling around, folding her wings down as though to dive.

"Harker, *stay!*" a command rang out, the unfamiliar voice of the stranger who claimed the ability to save us. I ignored him.

I leaped off the web, knees bending as I landed on the grav-board. I kicked it into gear, my body suddenly feeling twice as heavy as I surged upward. I heard the unfamiliar voice again, calling out, "*Harker! I will leave you behind!*" as the light around me changed, taking on a purplish hue.

Fine, I thought, *but I'm not leaving her.* I could see Josephine a few yards above me, spread-eagled to slow her fall. If I could get to her before Lady Indigo did—

Time seemed to slow like that; Josephine falling toward me, Lady Indigo right behind her, skeletal wings folded back to minimize resistance. Josephine tucked her arms and legs in close to her body in an attempt to fall faster. I reached for her.

She was backlit by a flash of light, bright red and soundless, like the explosion of a small star. The force propelled her forward, her head snapping back awkwardly at the sudden motion. Then my arms were around her, and I pushed off the grav-board, jumping backward, flying (falling?) back to our comrades. Lady Indigo was nowhere to be seen, and that familiar purple light was seeping in around the edges of my vision. As we fell closer and closer to it, I heard that voice again, screaming, *"Leave her!"*

I held Josephine tighter, falling into the light. She was limp as a rag doll in my arms.

CHAPTER SEVEN

I HIT THE GROUND hard, on my back, my arms still wrapped around Josephine, cradling her protectively against my chest. The air left my lungs, stars exploding in the corners of my vision—but I could still make out the tip of that circuitry-bladed sword as it was leveled at my face.

"I told you to leave her," the boy who wasn't Acacia snapped. All I could do was glare, half turned to protect Josephine with my body.

"We don't leave our own behind," Joeb said calmly, coming up to put a hand on the boy's shoulder. "Please, explain yourself."

The boy shrugged Joeb's hand off, which gave me the opportunity to scoot back from the tip of his blade. I leaned up against a wall, registering dimly that we were back at InterWorld Beta. There were more than a few of us in the room right now, but at the moment, I only cared about one.

"Josephine," I murmured, propping her head against my shoulder and touching her cheek. She didn't respond, though her eyes were open. I felt my breath catch, fear clutching at my stomach. This wasn't happening.

"I'm Avery Jones, Agent of TimeWatch," the boy answered, and I slowly looked up. "And if you don't leave your own behind, explain why my people had to find and fix *him*."

He gestured with the hand that wasn't holding the sword, and at first I had no idea what he was indicating. There were several of my team members standing there, as they had been when we'd arrived. Jo's white angel wings, some of them still wrapped firmly with bandages, stood out starkly against the gray-silver walls. Next to her was Josef, who also stood out due to his massive size. J'r'ohoho was on the floor before them, not moving, and kneeling next to him was a Walker who looked almost exactly like me, tears on his face as he gripped the centaur's shoulder.

"J/O," I breathed, a jolt going through me. The last time I'd seen J/O, he'd been trying to kill me. Now he was crying, head bowed over J'r'ohoho's body.

"We found him wandering through the timestream," Avery accused. "Who left him there, exactly?"

"I had no choice," I snapped, recalling vividly the feeling of Acacia's hand on my shoulder, the way all the strength left my body as she took me through time against my will. "Acacia—"

I got no further. He took two steps forward before I could react, the tip of his sword pressing against my lower lip. The blade was warm against my skin.

"Say her name again, and see what happens," he said, his voice low and angry.

I should have stayed still. I should have pulled back slowly and answered calmly, and I knew it. Instead, I was on my feet almost before I knew what I intended to do, batting the sword away and closing the distance between us. My hand found the material of his vest, and I hauled him closer to me.

"Whatever she may be to you, *Acacia*," I said deliberately, "is also a friend of *mine*."

His eyes, which were violet like hers, flashed green for a second. Whatever that meant or whatever he'd been about to do, I never found out. Joeb pulled us apart, fixing me with a stern, hard look. Out of the corner of my eye, I saw J/O get to his feet, wiping the tears from his face.

"I'm sorry, Joey," he said, one of the few times I'd ever heard him apologize to me. "I was completely reprogrammed. I didn't . . . I wouldn't have . . ."

"I know," I said, still glaring at Avery. "I know you wouldn't have. You okay now?"

"Yes. Fully operational. TimeWatch found me and cleaned out the virus."

"You're welcome," Avery said snidely. I fought the urge to throw a punch, Joeb's hand against my chest providing a comforting measure of stability. "If that's settled, I suggest you figure out what to do with her." He gestured over my shoulder, and I bristled.

"She's one of *us*, and not your concern."

"Not *her*," he said, not even sparing a glance past me to where Josephine lay. "The Agent of HEX."

"What are you talking about?" Joeb asked, still trying to keep the peace.

"You didn't think it odd that she allowed your escape so easily?"

"That was *easy*?"

"Compared to what one of her power is capable of, yes. Did she not take out several of your number before I came to your rescue?"

We glared at each other, my anger struggling with what little common sense I was holding on to. One thought made itself known amid the fury I was fighting to keep under control.

"You knew that was going to happen," I said.

"Of course I did," he responded, and I very nearly went for him again.

"Why didn't you stop it?" I yelled, pressing against Joeb's hand on my shoulder.

"I'm a Time Agent, Joseph Harker, I have bigger problems. It's not *my* job to police the Altiverse. It's *yours*, and it's a job you're not going to be able to do at all if you don't stop being an idiot and *listen*," he snapped. "You think you know best? You think you made a clean getaway, even though I told you to leave her?"

"Joe," came a whisper from behind me, and I forgot all about Avery Jones and TimeWatch as I went immediately to kneel by Josephine's side. "He's right," she breathed, a mere hint of a sound, so faint I had to put my ear right down to her lips. "She's with me. I can hear her singing in my head. . . ."

"We'll fix it," I assured her, but she made a small sound of negation.

"Can't. I know what she did . . . what happened to the others. I know what she knows. I know she's coming here."

"She can't come through time—no one but the Time Agents and Hue can!" I looked back to Avery for confirmation, but he was shaking his head.

"Weren't you listening to a thing she said? She knows how to sense you, and how to drain you. That's how she killed the others." Avery gestured behind him, to J'r'ohoho and the other Walkers lying too still on the cool metal floor. "She stole away their lives, and that's—"

"What she's doing to me," Josephine whispered. "I can feel it. I can feel the others. . . ."

I stared at her, at a loss. All I could think of was that house I hadn't grown up in, the one with the portrait of the redheaded, freckle-faced girl and the woman with the prosthetic arm whose daughter would never come home. Avery was saying something else, but I only tuned back in to one specific part.

". . . is how she'll track her through time. She's created a soul link, and that means she can follow it anywhere, even here." Something tugged at my memory, but Josephine twitched beside me, her hand tightening in mine.

"Avery's right," she said, and out of the corner of my eye I saw him turn toward us. "You can't let her, Joe. He's right. She's coming here. You have to fly. Fly away."

"We can't fly yet, Josephine," I whispered. "You know that. We don't have power."

She looked past me. A smile tilted up the corners of her mouth, barely. "I have power," she said.

I felt another jolt of adrenaline break out a cold sweat all over my body. "No," I said, putting as much force as I could into it without growling at her.

"You told me . . . You said they use us to power their ships."

I pulled back from her, feeling like I'd been punched. "No way," I managed. I felt sick. "I am not . . . I won't . . . !" I faltered, unable to even find the words I needed. She wanted me to use her to power the ship, like HEX and Binary used us? She didn't understand what she was asking me. She hadn't seen what I'd seen.

She was my first ever recruit. I couldn't lose her.

"I want to," she insisted, her voice stronger than it had been a moment ago. "I want to see InterWorld fly."

"The idea has merit," Avery said from behind me, and even Joeb looked like he might be considering letting me hit Avery.

"You don't understand," Joeb began, but Avery shook his head.

"Like hell I don't. I know exactly what she's asking you to do, and I'm telling you, it's not a bad idea."

"You're insane!" I shouted, getting back to my feet. "You want me to use her like HEX does, then? Boil her down to nothing, keep her in a jar? We don't have a cryochamber here to freeze her like Binary does, but I'm sure we can build one! Hell, we'll install it next to the showers, put it to everyday use!"

"Joey," Joeb murmured, but I ignored him.

"I won't use one of my own like that, no matter what TimeWatch says."

I expected Avery to get mad, but he just calmly put away his sword, little flashes of electricity sparking blue as it slid into the metal sheath. "This is not a directive from Time-Watch."

"Even if it was, TimeWatch can kiss my—"

"Joey!" Joeb was looking at me seriously, arms folded across his chest. He raised an eyebrow, glancing back down to Josephine, who was breathing shallowly, gaze fixed on us.

Everyone else was watching me, too, Jo with her white wings folded around herself in comfort, Josef with tears on his face. Jakon's furry ears were cocked back uncertainly, her expression sad. I turned my back on all of them, glaring at Joeb.

"I *won't*," I said.

"I would," said Jo, from behind me. "If I had a choice. If I was dying, and I could be part of InterWorld forever . . . I would."

"So would I," Josef rumbled.

"I'd donate my circuits and power core," J/O admitted. "I wouldn't be using them, and I'd give anything to keep Inter-World up and running."

More voices spoke up from around me, adding their general agreement. Not everyone spoke up, but no one said they disagreed. Not one of them.

"You have mere minutes, Harker," Avery said, though he was looking at Josephine rather than me. "The HEX witch will find her way here unless you act."

"Wouldn't . . . wouldn't binding her to the ship keep that link?" I asked, grasping desperately at straws. "Wouldn't Lady Indigo be able to track us, then?"

"I can break the link," Avery said.

"Then why don't you? Just—"

"Because breaking it will kill her," he snapped. "And

despite what you think of me, I am unwilling to do so without her permission."

The room was holding its breath. Everyone was watching me as I stood there in silence, staring at the floor. I had no idea why, but I suddenly remembered when I'd first come to InterWorld with Jay's body. I'd woken up in the infirmary and seen Jay's funeral from the window, and after that the Old Man had come in to see me. He'd talked to me about InterWorld and our purpose and our enemies and our duties. He'd talked about our oath and our values and he'd told me when my classes started, but that wasn't what I found myself remembering. It was when I'd asked if he blamed me for Jay's death.

Yes, he'd said. *Of course I do.*

"J/O," I said, and the cyborg version of me looked up. "Can one of the PLSS units in the infirmary be modified to hook up to a transducer?"

"I think so," he said.

"Figure it out, fast. Josef, go get one and bring it to the engine room." I didn't even have to look to know the huge version of me was doing as told. I could feel his footsteps *thump, thump, thump* down the hall as he left, like a heartbeat.

Josephine looked up at me from where she was propped up weakly against the wall. "I want to do this," she whispered.

Joeb and Avery walked behind me as I carried Josephine

down the hall to the engine room, ignoring the pain in my injured shoulder. I could hear everyone else following, the footsteps of thirty or so of me echoing in the dead ship.

I don't remember much from the moment the decision was made to when I saw Josef bring in the PLSS—one of the portable life support systems we kept in the infirmary. I know at some point I'd sent a few others to get a cot, which was what Josephine was currently laid out upon next to the machines. She was paler than we usually were, her freckles standing out starkly against her skin. I imagined I was beginning to see the bones beneath, like Lady Indigo's translucent skin. She was sweating and she kept telling us to hurry up so we could get this over with.

Once we'd gotten her set up on the cot, Avery had knelt next to her. He hadn't moved since, and she was smiling faintly as they spoke in low tones. He was holding her hand. It seemed odd—hadn't they just met?—but I had other things to worry about right now.

"That should do it," J/O said, his voice subdued as he stepped back from the machinery. "The PLSS is hooked up to the solar power grid, so it'll run. Theoretically, if she . . . when she . . ."

"Dies," I said. The younger version of me blanched.

"When that happens while she's hooked up to the PLSS, it'll store an imprint of her and autopulse to act as a defibrillator. I have the pulse wired into the transducer instead."

"Fine," I said. "Get me Jai." I turned away, making myself go over to Josephine. I ignored Avery. "You don't have to do this," I said, and she made a faint sound that might have been a laugh.

"Shut up," she told me. "You're being a wimp. What kind of leader are you, anyway?"

"A bad one," I answered. "I keep letting my people get killed."

"Get better at it," she said. "I'm going to make this ship fly. You better keep it in the air, got it?" She was white as a ghost now, shadows ringing her eyes. Her lips were dark with blood from where she'd been biting them.

"We're ready, Joey." Joeb's voice came from behind me, right before I heard the PLSS flare to life.

"I keep running but she knows," Josephine whispered, looking up at Avery. "I keep hiding, but she can find me anywhere. I'm the flame to her moth. Mother Moth . . ."

"Shh," he said, and smoothed a hand over her hair. "She won't find you, Josie. I promise."

I frowned, glancing sidelong at him as he stood. He ignored me, stepping out of the way as J/O came over to hook her up to the machines.

"Jai?" I said.

"Present," said the familiar voice, and the calm,

brown-skinned version of me stepped over to Josephine's other side.

"You're the magic guy," I said, "And this is some serious magic. I don't care how it works or how you do it, but your job is to make sure nothing goes wrong. Make sure the link is gone, and help guide her to . . . wherever. J/O, make sure the transducer works right."

Jai shifted me a thoughtful glance, but said nothing. He nodded, holding one hand out above Josephine and closing his eyes.

"Avery—"

"I know what I'm doing," came the rough response, the dark-haired boy moving to stand at the edge of the cot. He put a hand on the hilt of his sword. "Back up."

There was that cold hard knot in my stomach again, though I wasn't sure if it was from anger or fear. I took a step back, watching as Jai focused.

"I can sense the link," Jai said. "It is intact, and strong."

"Show them," Avery said, and Jai concentrated.

At first, nothing happened. Then I saw a glint, like something above us caught the light, just for a moment. It was there and then gone, then there was another, and another; like the thin threads of a spiderweb glinting in the sun. There were maybe ten of them that I could see, tinged vaguely with red and all in a bundle. They started at Josephine, wrapped loosely around her, and arced upward. I looked around, trying to find their source, but they were nonlinear and scattered, winding around all of us and slowly tightening, like they were being pulled taut.

"She's coming," Josephine whispered. I heard the click of Avery's sword as he tightened his hand around the hilt.

"Josephine," I said suddenly. "There's something I never did."

All eyes turned to me.

"Repeat after me," I said. "I, Josephine Harker."

Her gaze found mine, and she gave a tiny half smile. "I, Josephine Harker."

"Understanding that there must be balance in all things, hereby declare that I shall do all in my power to defend and protect the Altiverse from those who would harm it or bend it to their will. That I will do everything I can to support and stand for InterWorld and the values it embodies."

She repeated it, word for word, though her voice was barely above a whisper by the end and her knuckles were white where her hands gripped the side of the cot. The threads above her blurred as my eyes watered, and for a moment, I was able to see them all clearly.

"Welcome to InterWorld," I whispered. My voice sounded bitter even to me.

Avery moved, so suddenly I almost missed it, whipping

his sword from the sheath and striking in the same motion. The circuitry blade cut cleanly through the strands that wound around us all and I saw one, just before it fell, going straight through the heart of Avery Jones.

INTERLOG

I didn't want this mission in the first place.

I know that sounds whiny, and I am not trying to complain, but I need to find Acacia. I understand that we can't spare any Agents for her; we've got our hands full trying to keep the Techs in line. I know that.

But she's my little sister, damn it. She's all I've got. Even now . . . Damn him. And Josephine, too.

I didn't want this mission, but I took it because it would put me into contact with Joseph Harker. From what I can tell, he's the last person to have seen Acacia before she vanished. I wanted the chance to question him, at the very least, even if it wasn't part of this specific job. I was supposed to be bringing the infected Walker back to his correct timeline, but that proved more difficult than I thought.

Acacia shouldn't have sent him to InterWorld's End. That's a point far in the future, so far it had no bearing on him. He had no business being there. Into the future, sure, off to a remote location where no one but the Techmaturges could have gotten to him . . . but my sister decided otherwise, apparently.

Technically, it was Harker's own future path. Thousands of years after his death, of course, but still on the same timeline. The MDLF showing up to bring him back through the future was unexpected, though I have to wonder if my sister hadn't taken that into account.

She spoke highly of him in her reports, though I have to admit I'm not overly impressed.

He's rash, and he doesn't follow directions. He doesn't listen. I told him to leave Josephine behind, and instead he brought her onto the ship, compromising his entire mission. The HEX witch would have made her way on board, if I hadn't acted. If I hadn't killed Josie.

It wasn't supposed to happen that way.

Damn this mission.

CHAPTER EIGHT

IT DIDN'T HAPPEN IMMEDIATELY. To be perfectly honest, it was fairly anticlimactic. The threads faded, their broken ends sparking blue with electricity, flashing like little fireflies before they vanished. Josephine's hands slowly relaxed where they'd gripped the edges of the cot. She took a breath, then another, and then she didn't. The PLSS gave a pulse, made a sound kind of like *dzzzt!* and then a little green light on the transducer powered on.

"It's working," J/O said. He sounded timid, as though he was afraid to break the silence. I saw Jai look at Avery and nod. The Agent of TimeWatch nodded back, then looked down at Josephine's body. He looked at her for a long moment, then turned and walked out without a word.

"Make sure it stays working," I said. "As soon as we have enough power, give us a jump and get us moving." J/O looked startled.

"I—I've never . . ."

"You can plug into the main console, can't you?"

"Theoretically, but . . ."

"Then do that. It's not like flying a jet or anything—you're not gonna flip us. Just program the coordinates," I said. He still looked uncertain, but I was already heading to the door. "Jo!"

She glanced up from the small throng of people still huddled around the bodies of the unmoving Walkers. I realized with a start that they'd brought them with us as we all trouped into the engine room—and *then* I realized I was going to have to figure out what to do with their bodies. We couldn't just . . . keep them.

"Are they all dead?" I asked as she fell into step with me. I was surprised at the steadiness of my voice.

"Yes," she said quietly.

"Who?"

"J'r'ohoho, Jenna, and Jerem."

I took a breath, shoving it aside. I'd mourn them later. "Okay. Gather everyone to the mess for me."

"Okay. Everyone?"

"Except J/O, he's getting the ship online." I paused, then reconsidered. "And Jai, leave him with J/O." I was *pretty* sure that J/O was totally fine now, but all I had was Avery's word for it . . . and speaking of words, he and I needed to have some.

"What should I tell him?"

"Tell him to watch over the bodies." Jai was smart; he'd get it.

"Okay. Joey," she said, as we started to go down different corridors. She paused. "Don't screw up," she warned, the ghost of a smile passing over her face.

I nodded, and we went our separate ways. It may have seemed harsh, but that was Jo's style—and her telling me not to mess up was more than a warning. It was a declaration. It meant she would follow me, and so would everyone else. It meant I *couldn't* mess up, because everyone was depending on me now.

It was something I was already painfully aware of.

"Hey," I called, as I rounded another corner to see Avery. He was standing in front of the Wall, our memorial to the fallen. It had started outside the infirmary, no one knew when or by whom, and back on InterWorld Alpha I was used to it spanning one side of a long hallway. Here, on this InterWorld so far in the future, it extended out into three different halls at least.

He shifted slightly at my voice, though he didn't turn. He didn't seem to be looking at anything in particular, just the Wall in general, which had everything from bits of seashells to silly doodles to jewelry to feathers and teeth from species I'd never heard of. There was a lot to look at, and each thing held personal significance for a Walker long dead.

"Come to interrogate me?" he asked as I drew closer.

"Give me a reason not to," I said. "Tell me exactly why you're here." He turned his head to look at me, his violet eyes cold.

"I was returning your cyborg."

"What else?"

He lifted his chin slightly, considering me. After a moment, he said, "I am fulfilling the mission of another Agent who is currently LAS."

"LAS?"

He glanced away for a moment, as though I was trying his patience. "Lost at sea. An equivalent term for you, I suppose, would be MIA."

"Acacia," I said. I'd been through so much in the last twenty minutes that the thought of her being missing didn't upset me as much as it maybe should have. "You don't know where she is?"

"I had hoped that you would," he said, looking at me coolly, "since you're the last person on record to see her."

"What do you mean, 'on record'?"

"That is classified and none of your business, and I won't explain it."

"Fine," I said, matching his tone. "Then, since you're here in her place, and I'm here in the Old—in Captain Harker's place, I'm going to tell you the same thing he told her: You have prime clearance, as long as you're escorted at all times.

That escort will be me. You spend one second out of my sight, and I will consider you a threat to this ship and the people on it."

"Fine," was all I got in response. I should have expected it.

I turned to leave again, assuming he'd follow me. He did, though not without another lingering glance back to the Wall. I paused, curiosity getting the better of me.

"You called her 'Josie,' like you knew her. Why?"

If I'd thought he was cold before, the look he gave me now almost froze me where I stood. "That," he said, his fingers brushing over the hilt of his sword, "is also none of your business."

We looked at each other for a long moment, and then I turned my back on him and started for the mess hall.

There were twenty-five of us total in the mess hall, since Jai and J/O were still in the engine room, and we'd lost four of us since the last time I'd done a head count.

Four of us, in the last twenty minutes.

I stood on a table, facing the room at large, the gathered Walkers standing or sitting around me. The room was a wreck; it looked like it had been used as a choke point for whatever it was that had attacked InterWorld. Tables were overturned and had been used as barricades; chairs were discarded and broken; various bits of metal and machinery that had probably once been weapons were scattered about the floor. I took it all in, trying to recapture what those last moments would have been like, and trying not to let the hopelessness of the situation overtake me. If this was to be InterWorld's end, what point was there in what I was doing now?

It was quite simple, really. This was what I knew. It was what I'd been trained for—hell, for all I could tell, it was what I'd been born for. Me, and every other version of me there was. I couldn't *not* do it.

But, God, that was so hard to remember when I was standing there, looking at their faces. Most of them were tear streaked, dirty, and tired. Some were bruised or scratched, and they all looked as beaten down as I felt. I wondered if this was how the Old Man felt when he spoke to us after a failed mission. I wonder if he'd trained himself not to feel anything at all.

"I'm sure a lot of you are wondering what the hell happened," I started, deciding to get right to the point. "Near as I can tell, after the first group we sent with Josephine and Hue—my mudluff friend—arrived safely here, the large expenditure of Walker energy caught the attention of a HEX agent known as Lady Indigo. She was ready for the second group when we tried to Walk, and pulled us into the Nowhere-at-All. Three of us were killed.

"Josephine Harker was a Walker I recruited and trained, and though she was new to Walking, she was very, very good at it. She used this to her advantage and slipped away while the rest of us were captured. I didn't sense her, and neither did Lady Indigo. She, along with TimeWatch Agent Avery Jones, came to our rescue. It is because of them that we escaped as we did. However, Lady Indigo formed an energy link with Josephine that would have allowed her to track us here, even through time. We severed that link, which means we are safe from her for now. Unfortunately, Josephine was killed in the process." As hard as all of that had been to say, it was nothing compared to what I had to get through next.

"Her last wish was to have her spirit used to jump-start this ship." A murmur went through the crowd from those who hadn't been present for that discussion; I fought to control the wave of guilt that swept over me, to ignore the voice in my head that told me I didn't deserve to be standing before them like some kind of leader. I'd let us get captured, gotten several of us killed, and then used my first recruit just like our enemies would have.

Forcing myself to continue, I said, "J/O and Jai are overseeing the process of bringing power back to the ship. Once we're up and running, we'll see how far the engines will take us. In the meantime, our priorities are twofold. First, we have to get the ship in order. This is our temporary base of operations until we can get back to InterWorld Prime, which brings me to our second goal.

"When last I saw it, InterWorld Prime—or InterWorld

Alpha, as I've been calling it—had been detected by a HEX ship. They've thrown the engines into overdrive and punched it, but HEX is right on their tail. This means they can't stop, which means they can't help us. Everyone on that ship, including the Old Man, is trapped until we find a way to help them."

I let that sink in, already dividing them up into groups in my head, sorting out who would be best for what. It was surprisingly easy; I knew my team and their capabilities, and I was passingly familiar with a handful of the others here. Joeb knew many of them better, so I could work with him to place people into teams. By the time the murmuring had died down again, I'd figured out the people I needed.

"Joeb, Jo, and Josef, with me. Everyone else, get to the living quarters and pick a bunk. They're all pretty messed up; you're responsible for cleaning yours out, but *don't* just move any junk or debris into another room. Take it all the way out to the courtyard. You three," I said to Joeb, Jo, and Josef, who'd stepped forward. "The Old Man's office. You, too," I told Avery, who had been leaning one shoulder against the wall, arms folded, listening quietly. He fell into step behind us, and as we left I heard the others start filing out toward the living quarters.

It still boggled my mind that people were just . . . doing what I told them. No one had said a word nor asked a question nor wondered *why I was giving orders*. Granted, I was the only one who currently knew everything that was going on . . . which led me to the third part of our mission, the one I hadn't told anyone about. Yet.

I'd chosen the Old Man's office because it was a secure room with one entrance, one we could see from any angle. I still wasn't taking any chances with J/O, and I'd already learned my lesson about the possibility of traitors in our midst. The only other one of us I was unsure of was Avery Jones, because he *wasn't* one of us, but it was better to keep him with me than let him wander around unsupervised.

"Joey . . ." Jo paused in the doorway to the Old Man's receiving room. It still existed in my memory as the personalized, semicozy office space the Old Man's assistant Josetta had always kept, not as the wreck it was now. There had been comfortable, plush waiting chairs and a soft, colorful rug, and Josetta's desk had been covered with knickknacks and multicolored Post-its. It had been one of the few rooms on Base, aside from our own individual ones, that showed any sort of personality.

Now it was covered in a layer of fine dust and ash, the rug long since disintegrated, the desk overturned, and the chairs rotted. Jo stood in the doorway, her wings fluffed up slightly in alarm. "Why here?" she asked.

"Because it's the closest thing we have to soundproof,"

I said, ushering Joeb, Josef, and Avery into the Old Man's office. "And I have things to say that can't leave this room. Come on."

She hesitated a moment more, then visibly steeled herself and crossed the threshold. I knew how she felt; like we were intruding, standing in shoes we had no right to even think of filling.

I'd been feeling like that since I first got here.

"I called in you three for a few reasons," I began. "First, I trust you. Second, I need you." I looked at Joeb.

"Joeb, you and Jai are the only senior officers I have, and I'll need Jai here for a while. You have more experience than any of us with extracting Walkers, and that's what I need you to do. Put together a team or do it solo, it's your call, but I need you to go get more of us. As many as you can find. You'll need Hue to sense them; I'll show you how."

He nodded, seeming unsurprised by the request and (to my relief) unbothered by the notion of working with my mudluff friend. Many of us (including myself, not that it had stopped me) had been taught from the beginning that MDLFs were incredibly dangerous, so most of my teammates had never quite grown to trust Hue.

"Josef, you're in charge of clearing out the debris. We need clear hallways, and access to the equipment lockers. I have no idea what, if anything, is in there; it's completely blocked, Josephine . . . and I weren't able to get in." I paused for a moment, a half second after her name. I couldn't help it. Maybe if we'd been able to get more equipment out of the lockers, she would have had more of a chance against Lady Indigo. Maybe if I'd done anything differently . . .

Josef nodded amiably, his curly head barely brushing the ceiling. "I can probably move most of it myself," he said.

"Get J/O to help you if you can't, as soon as he has the ship up and running." He nodded again, and I turned to Jo. She was getting the worst job, but I knew she'd be the best at it. She was practical and organized, and sometimes seemed to have more common sense than everyone else put together.

"Jo, I need you to put together several teams in charge of getting the facilities up and running. The kitchens, lavatories, and infirmary are the priorities. We managed with two of us, but there are over twenty now, and with Joeb's help"—I glanced to him briefly—"there should be more. Soon." Both Joeb and Jo nodded seriously. As I'd hoped, Jo had accepted the task without complaint. I made a mental note to make it up to her later, somehow.

If there was a later.

"Okay," I said, taking a breath. "Joeb gets first priority on Walkers, then Josef, then Jo. Work it out."

They looked at me, then each other. There was a moment of silence, then Jo went back out to Josetta's waiting room, where I could hear her digging around for anything that might be useful for taking notes. Josef nodded to me and followed. Joeb stopped to give my uninjured shoulder a careful squeeze, then went out after them.

"Not bad," Avery said. "You almost sound like a leader."

"Glad you think so," I replied, "because you're about to get debriefed."

He raised an eyebrow.

"You said your people found J/O wandering through the timestream, and you cleaned out the virus and brought him here. Tell me more."

He folded his arms.

Just when I thought he wasn't going to answer me (and I didn't have any idea what I intended to do if that were the case—I could threaten him, but I wasn't sure I could take him in a fight even were I at the top of my game, which I most certainly was not . . .), he shrugged and spoke. "My people picked up an anomaly in the navigation system."

"What does that mean, exactly?"

"It's on a need to know basis," he said. "And you don't."

"Fair," I admitted, nodding for him to continue.

"Your friend was tripping all kinds of alarms, wandering around through time like that. Not only did we need to stop him, we needed to figure out how he was doing it. You Walkers can't sail those storms, at least not without the help of an MDLF."

Though I didn't like the obnoxious way he said "you

Walkers," I had to admit he was right.

"Did you find out how he was managing it when you cleaned out the virus?"

Avery hesitated, probably deciding whether or not this counted as "need to know." "Yes, but it was programming he shouldn't have had. We determined that it was a supplementary drive installed in his processing center."

"You mean, they added new software to him?"

"More like they added the hardware required to support the software upgrades, but, yes. We removed it along with the virus."

I was a bit irritated at everyone's apparently fishing around in J/O's guts (or circuits, whatever) without his permission, but I understood why it had been done. Binary had done it because, hey, they're the bad guys. TimeWatch had done it because they had the monopoly on time travel, and wanted to keep it that way.

Not that they were doing a very good job—and not that I was ruling out the possibility of them being bad guys, mind you. My friendship with Acacia aside, I had yet to meet one single Agent of TimeWatch who didn't completely rub me the wrong way. *Including* Acacia.

"There've been two, so far," I said.

"What?"

"J/O, and Lady Indigo. That's two people in recent

memory who have been able to do something we thought was impossible. Fixing on essence and tracking through time, specifically."

Avery narrowed his eyes. "I said the witch created a link. I never said she fixed on Josephine's essence."

"But that's what she did, isn't it?"

"Yes," Avery admitted, watching me closely. "What do you know about time signatures and essence waves?"

"Absolutely nothing," I said, and he looked both doubtful and suspicious. "I mean it. I have no clue what you're talking about."

"You knew enough to call it 'essence,'" he accused.

"That's what J/O said when he was tracking us through time. He said he'd fixed on our essence. Acacia said that's what the Techmaturges did." If I thought he'd looked suspicious before, he looked downright accusatory now.

"Did she," he said. It wasn't a question.

"Yes," I said. "But if it makes you feel any better, I didn't hear that name from her. She was as surprised as you are that I knew about them."

"And where did you hear about them?"

"That's need to know," I said, admittedly a bit more smugly than I meant to. I heard a subtle *click clack* coming from the hilt of his sword as he shifted his stance. "But regardless, I first heard the word 'essence' used like that from J/O. He said he was fixed on our essences, and could follow us anywhere. Binary agents can't normally do that. Neither can HEX, as far as I was aware, but you didn't seem at all surprised that Lady Indigo had created a link like that."

"The witch had grown her powers beyond those of a normal HEX agent during her time in the Nowhere-at-All. It is surprising that she was able to do what she did, but not impossible. Especially not with the powers of those she'd absorbed."

I winced at the word "absorbed." Those had been my friends. "Fine. So, she could do it because of that, and J/O could do it because he'd been programmed to."

"Correct."

"But he can't, anymore."

"Right."

"And he's completely okay, now."

"Yes. He retains the memories but not the programming. You can trust him as much as you ever did."

"Great." I paused. "How much can I trust you?"

Avery smirked.

"If you say that's 'need to know,' I swear I will eject you from this ship into an erupting volcano," I warned. "I know of several exact times and places, believe me. Pompeii is particularly nice this time of year."

"It *is* need to know. Fortunately, you do." His smirk faded and he sighed. "You may trust that I have no ill intentions toward you or anyone on this ship. My mission, in fact, is to help you. As was my sister's."

It was the first time he'd acknowledged the relationship between him and Acacia, though I wasn't entirely surprised—they did look so much alike. I was more confused with the knowledge of what her mission—and now, his—had been. "Help me *what*?"

He gave another little sigh, as though I was trying his patience again. "You may recall that HEX and Binary have joined forces to unleash some kind of Multiverse-reshaping horror, do you not?"

"FrostNight."

"Yes. It has already begun, and I am here to help you stop it."

I felt my stomach sink into my shoes. "It's been destroying worlds this whole time?" I said. I had been prepared for this, of course. Everything I had been doing since I left Mr. Dimas had been preparing for this—I'd been gathering up Walkers for this very reason, to take the fight to Binary and HEX, but some small part of me had still been holding out hope that *maybe* Acacia and I had managed to stop it before it was released.

"Yes," Avery said. "It has." Despite his words, his tone wasn't at all accusatory, just matter-of-fact, which still kind of grated on me. I shoved the irritation aside. There were more important things to worry about than my ego.

"Okay. So, how *do* we stop it?"

Avery paused, and for the first time I saw his mask of composure slip an inch. He looked uncertain, and worried. "We are not sure. This is the only timestream in which this has ever happened. If there had been others and it had been stopped before it could complete its purpose, we would have record of the events. If it had come into existence and not been stopped, there would not be any . . . *anything*."

That took me a moment to decipher, but I was fairly confident I got it. "You mean, if FrostNight was ever completed it would have eradicated *everything*, including TimeWatch."

"Yes. We would not exist, had it ever happened."

"So . . . what you're saying is, you work for an organization that has record of everything that has ever happened and ever will happen, and you have no idea how to stop this thing."

There was the sound of metal clicking against metal as Avery tightened his grip on his sword. I inched one foot back defensively, but the motion seemed to be more of a nervous habit than a threat. I was oddly comforted by the discovery of this quirk; it made him seem a little more human.

"Yes," he said reluctantly. "That is what I'm saying."

I took a deep breath.

I didn't know what else to say—what could I say? None of us, anywhere, knew how to stop FrostNight, and yet we were the only ones who had a chance. Luckily, I was saved from trying to figure it out. There was a sudden shudder and a hollow moan, and the high-pitched whine of long-unused machinery. The dim room was flooded with light as the autoillumination system kicked in, and we both squinted in the sudden brilliance. Through the open doorway, I heard the cheers and whistles of the other Walkers as InterWorld hummed to life around us, like it was waking suddenly from a nightmare.

We stood there in silence, looking at the walls, the lights, and each other. I couldn't help thinking that this was Josephine, all around us, here but gone. Not even a soul or consciousness, just the spark that had started the flame.

This ship was her vigil, the candle at her funeral. The spark was gone, but the flame remained. And I would make sure it burned for as long as I could.

I don't know what I was expecting or hoping for, but Avery didn't break the sudden silence, nor did he look like he was going to. I don't know if he was thinking about Josephine or Acacia or something else entirely, and I had no real desire to ask him. I finally settled for, "What now?"

He shrugged. "Now, I suppose you continue on with your plans, while I attempt to facilitate them."

"Meaning you're here to help."

"Yes."

"Great. Can you do anything useful?"

He leveled me with a long look, but answered, "I can help

your cyborg friend make sure this ship stays running and expand your time parameters so you may reach your desired timestream."

"Great," I said again. "Let's go do that, then."

I turned and left the Old Man's office. I could hear Avery's footsteps echoing hollowly behind mine as he followed.

CHAPTER NINE

I HAD MISSED THE way the working ship felt beneath my feet. It wasn't something I'd noticed until it was gone, but you could feel the hum of the engines through the floor no matter where you were. It was like standing next to a washer or dryer when it was on—a vibration against your feet so faint you barely felt it. I hadn't realized it until I'd stood on an InterWorld with no power, the floor cold and hard and dead beneath me.

Now it was thrumming again, alive and itching to fly. I felt it the moment I stepped into the engine room; the console was on, all the lights and dials and digital readouts blinking and humming and waiting. Still, I stayed there only for a moment after I escorted Avery back to J/O. I couldn't make myself look at the cots lining the back, the still forms occupying them all covered in sheets.

Instead, I went to the Wall.

Our monument to the fallen stood silent and still, not even a breeze sweeping through the hall to rustle the scraps of paper and feathers and fur. It extended a full three sectors past what I was used to; the InterWorld of the future had seen the deaths of thousands more of us.

I walked it for a time, up and down, memorizing the bits and pieces of people's lives, the scraps of feelings and hopes and dreams. They were all that remained of the comrades I'd never known, of those who'd fought and died long after whatever my end had been. I went back and forth, twice, from the infirmary to the remains of the automatic double doors that led out to what had once been the gardens. The long silver boxes that served as our coffins were still sitting out there, silent shapes in pools of sun, lined up in neat rows. I stepped out into the bright daylight and made myself open one.

Despite my fears, it was empty. I didn't know if the thin layer of dust that coated the bottom was all that remained of a person, if the boxes themselves transported the body within to somewhere else, or if these had never been filled in the first place. It had been so long since anyone had been here, it didn't matter. This place was all just ashes and dust.

The box was light enough to move, so I pulled it inside, to the hallway. I stared at the Wall for a long moment, thinking, and then I started taking it down.

Feathers, bits of glass, paper made thin and brittle with

age. Jewelry, faded pictographs and drawings, dusty and yellowed books, drawings so faint you could no longer tell what they were. I put them all into the long silver box carefully, and when that box was full, I pulled it back outside and got another one.

Some of the papers crumbled to dust in my hands, particularly when I got farther down the line, to the things that had been put up even longer ago. I cried for those papers, and the lost memories of people they had represented. Several times I stopped entirely, horrified at what I was doing, before I was filled once again with renewed determination. If ashes and dust and memories were all that remained of this InterWorld, it was our duty to fill it again with purpose. With hope.

The new recruits wouldn't see hope when they looked at this Wall. They wouldn't see hope when they saw the coffins outside, or how many of us had already died. These deaths weren't personal to them. They were a nightmare, a horror story, a holocaust long past. They were legends and myths, shoes too big to ever possibly fill. They were my ghosts now, mine alone.

Microchips and nanochips, pottery, threads and scraps of clothing and candy wrappers, a long red braid and bits of foreign currency. Everything went carefully into a silver coffin, and when I finally finished hours later, long after the sun had dipped behind the distant horizon, I was tired and hungry and blessedly not alone.

My team had joined me slowly, over the course of the day. Jakon, Josef, Jo, Jai, and J/O all came to help me put the memories to rest. Avery stood and watched, though he never said a word. He followed us silently, seeming to feel his help wouldn't be appreciated, though he looked like he understood. He even looked sympathetic as I took down my own monument to Jay, the dirt and rocks from the planet he'd died on that had spelled out "I'm sorry."

We worked in silence until it was done, and then they helped me carry the coffins to the Old Man's office. It seemed appropriate, somehow. We wouldn't be using it much, and it was big enough that they could all be pushed against the wall and there would still be space if we needed it.

We went back to the engine room. This time I made myself go to the bodies; there had been more coffins than we needed to hold all the stuff on the Wall. We each took one end of a cot, carried them back out to the gardens, and placed our fallen comrades one by one into the boxes. Avery and I went back together for Josephine.

When we were done, there were six long silver coffins sitting out in the courtyard. Four of them were occupied, and I had Josef and J/O take the remaining two into storage. Then Avery went to each of the boxes in turn and placed a hand on them. One by one, they glowed green and vanished, and I didn't bother to ask where he was sending them. The

Old Man had touched the coffins and made them vanish, too, and as far as I knew no one had ever asked him where they went. Perhaps they took the bodies home, wherever that was. Maybe they took us to a world where we could be born again, or to a planet that counted as heaven. Maybe it was a graveyard or a black hole. I didn't know, but it didn't matter. Death was death, and wherever we went afterward was something I would find out when my time came.

Avery paused by the fourth coffin, and he rested his hand on it for a moment longer than he had the other ones. I saw his lips move as he murmured something, too quietly for any of us to hear, and then he sent it off with the others. Luckily or not, I *had* been trained to read lips, and I echoed his words in a whisper as the final coffin glowed green and vanished.

"Good-bye, Josie," I said so quietly that the words were carried away on the wind.

My team and I stayed up in shifts that night, each of us taking a turn keeping an eye on Avery and J/O. I knew I was probably being paranoid, but I couldn't afford not to be.

Josef and a few of the Walkers he'd picked out slowly got the hallways cleared, and it became easier to get from place to place without having to crawl over rubble and debris. Jo, as I'd predicted, made short work of getting the public rooms ready; by nightfall the next day, all twenty-five or so of us had usable dorm rooms and the mess hall was, if not clean enough to eat off of, at least well on its way there.

The jump-start of the ship had gotten all the basic functions working, so we were able to open the storm shutters and get the ventilation working all through the ship. Auxiliary power kicked in on the second day, and InterWorld became self-sustaining once again. Avery, true to his word, expanded the time parameters in the warp drive, and we made the jump back into our own timeline without so much as a bit of turbulence.

Joeb brought in one recruit that second day, a sharp-looking girl who wore her red hair in a pixie cut. She was shorter and leaner than most of us middle-Arc Earth versions, and her eyes matched her hair. There was nothing really special about her—not from a magic- or science-heavy world, though she did have an affinity for fixing things. Her name was Jorily, and within the first few moments of meeting her I was of half a mind to make her the temporary quartermaster. After all, we still had an equipment locker full of what currently amounted to junk; now that we had power, some of the things in there could be recharged and possibly fixed. I told Joeb to go ahead and set her up down there, in addition to whatever basic training programs he was starting up.

I was operating out of the Old Man's office, which had *not* been my idea. Joeb and a few of the others had formed a team to clean it and get it more or less organized, and they'd insisted I run communications out of there.

"It's hooked up to all the main intercoms," Joeb had pointed out. "It's a secure location with more shields and protocols than we can even catalog, and it's automatic for most of us to go there in an emergency."

He'd had a lot more to say than that, mostly about how they needed someone to look to, and it wasn't so much about being in charge as it was *seeming* like I was in charge. I was a symbol, at least for the moment, and that meant I got to sit at a desk and divide our current numbers into teams and make lists of things that needed to be done. It meant, at least for a few days, that I had to stay put and recover, since I was still injured.

I was ready to go insane by the third day.

Joeb had brought three more recruits in, and I'd met them all. I'd given them the condensed version of what was happening, wished them luck, and sent them off to combat classes with Jakon and tactic lectures with Jo. I'd combed through any and all of the files that were still readable in the Old Man's office, trying to find *something—anything* that would give me some sort of direction, and I'd been doing this for two days straight before it occurred to me that though this may have been the Old Man's office in *my* time, I had no way of knowing who it had belonged to when the ship had been abandoned.

The thought stopped me dead. This whole time, I had been thinking of a new crew and a much older ship, of our same cause centuries in the future, and the same Captain.

This was, of course, impossible. But equally impossible was the image of someone else sitting at this desk, someone else giving us orders or sending out teams. The Old Man didn't have a second-in-command. He didn't have a lieutenant, or any officers aside from those he sent out on jobs or to recruit. It had always been just him. What would happen if he ever died?

The Old Man's office was the first place we went in an emergency, the first place we gathered in the event of *anything* that wasn't in the official handbook. It was where we went to get our missions and the first place we went—even before the infirmary, in some cases—after we returned. I couldn't imagine walking into this room and seeing anyone else.

But I was here. There were four or five people on this ship now who'd never even met the Old Man. People who'd only ever seen *me* sitting at this desk.

The thought was terrifying.

It was terrifying enough that I half stood from my chair before I even knew where exactly I was intending to go. I wanted *out*, away from this desk and its weight. I wanted to be training the recruits myself, or going out and getting them. This room was too big and too silent.

I sighed, then gingerly touched the tips of my fingers to the smooth surface of the desk. It flashed, then words started to crawl across it—Josetta's message to me, telling me to stay still and that she was sending someone to help. When I'd first come to this InterWorld, when TimeWatch had sent me here, I'd gone to the Old Man's desk and found the message. It was preprogrammed to react to the tracer in my bloodstream, which meant it would eventually go away. For now, though, I was stuck with seeing the message every time I touched it. I was stuck with the reminder that I was just a normal recruit who'd gotten in over his head.

I was still standing in front of the desk when one of the intercom lights blinked on. It was the private link from the engine room, where I'd left J/O, Jai, and Avery. "Joey," J/O's voice came over the speaker. He sounded rushed and worried. "Several of the alarm systems blipped at once, and Avery took off. He bolted out the door. I sent Jai after him, but—"

"What kind of alarms?"

"The radar blipped, then the proximity sensors."

"Activate any shields we have the power for—"

"There's nothing on the screen," J/O interrupted. "There's nothing to hit. The radar blipped once, but it's dark."

I stood there for a moment, waiting for a solution to come to me. I wasn't a captain, damn it, I didn't know what this meant or what to do in this situation. "And you said Avery just bolted?"

"Yeah. He—"

Whatever else J/O was saying was lost in a sudden, shrill

beep. There was a subtle rumble beneath my feet, small enough that I almost didn't feel it.

InterWorld was big enough that a small impact on one end of the ship wouldn't necessarily be felt on the other side, or even in the middle. The short, warning beep I'd heard from the engine room meant we'd hit something.

"Talk to me, J/O! What was that?"

"The radar's not— Wait, it's blinking in and out. It's too small to actually— Joey, it's headed right toward you!"

The rush of adrenaline I felt was compounded by the sudden crash behind me. I whirled just in time to see something fly by me, a rush of black and green. It slammed against the back wall of the Old Man's office with enough force that I felt the room shudder, and I coughed at the abrupt cloud of dust that welled up.

I'd insisted any weapons that had been scavenged or restored be given to the officers going out in the field; all I had on me was a switchblade I'd found in Josephine's backpack. Making sure all the teams were equipped had seemed like a perfectly sound idea at the time, but maybe I was about to regret that decision.

The dust was slowly clearing, though it didn't look like dust anymore. It was sort of pretty, like how the clouds would look on my world when the sun was setting. As if there was a light behind them, a purple light . . .

I ran over, skidding to my knees beside her. "Acacia!"

"Joey?" J/O's voice came though the speaker again, urgent and worried.

"I'm fine," I yelled, reaching down to clear some of the debris from her.

Acacia looked like she'd been through hell. Her clothing was marred by a hundred tiny cuts, dirty and singed in some places, like she'd fallen through a thornbush. (Or several. Some of them might have been on fire.) Her face and arms looked the same.

She was sprawled out on her back, a small indentation above her from where she'd obviously slammed into the wall and fallen. I risked a quick glance over my shoulder; part of the Old Man's doorway, already not in the best shape from whatever had cleared out the ship, was made even wider from where she'd clipped the side of it. I felt my blood run cold as I realized: somehow, the thing we'd hit was *Acacia*. There was no way she could have survived that impact.

A mere thread of a sound came from her, something too quiet to even be a whisper. I put a hand to her neck, feeling for a pulse. Miraculously, there was one. Even more miraculously, she slowly turned her head to look up at me. Her lips moved.

"What?" I leaned down, so close I could feel her breath against my ear.

"I'll pay for the damages," she murmured.

"I'm gonna kill you," I said, reaching out to touch her face.

"Get in line," said a voice from behind me, and I was summarily shoved aside as Avery knelt next to his sister, gathering her carefully into his arms.

"Ugh," she murmured, nose wrinkling in an expression I'd seen my own sister wear a thousand times, when looking at me. "Not *you*."

"Where in the abyss have you been, Cace?"

"Everywhere. Couldn't navigate. The stars were gone . . . they're going . . . They're . . ." She opened her eyes wide, sitting up in Avery's arms and reaching out to grab the front of my shirt. "The stars are going," she told me urgently, everything in her expression indicating this was of vital importance.

"Going where?" I asked.

"Dying," she said. "They're dying. FrostNight . . ."

Her grip on my shirt loosened, and her eyes lost focus. She passed out immediately, going limp against her brother.

"Sir?" another voice said behind me, as I felt the air shift from Jai's teleportation spell. Jai was sort of big on protocol, and he kept insisting he call me that as long as I was at the Old Man's desk. Ordinarily it bothered me; right now, I was focused on Acacia.

"Go ahead to the infirmary," I told him. "Tell them we have our first patient, then get back to the engine room. I've got things here."

He spared a brief glance at Avery, then nodded. Avery got

to his feet, cradling Acacia against him. He lifted her easily, paying no attention at all to Jai as he vanished. Now that they were both in the same place, the resemblance between them was more obvious—but even unconscious, Acacia had a fire to her that was different from her brother's quiet intensity.

"This way," I said, and turned to leave. I saw a hint of green in my peripheral vision. Instinct took over, and I whirled and grabbed for Avery. One hand closed around his forearm, the other going to Acacia's shoulder. Damned if I was going to let her vanish again.

"Let go, Harker."

"Where are you going?"

"Home."

"Why?"

"Because she needs medical attention, and my people are better equipped to give it than yours."

I couldn't argue with that, and I didn't want to. I wanted Acacia to be okay, even if it meant going back to TimeWatch and away from me—and for that reason, I hated what I was about to say.

"Your mission wasn't to rescue your sister. It was to help us stop FrostNight, and Acacia has information about FrostNight. She needs to stay here until I get that information."

Avery was already standing rigid, but he managed to straighten up even more as he stared at me. His eyes narrowed, and I felt his arm flex where I had a grip on his wrist.

If he hadn't had Acacia in his arms, he might have tried to throw me off him.

"Look," I said, trying to pitch my voice to be reasonable, "I'm worried about her, too. But you said yourself that Frost-Night would eradicate *everything*, including TimeWatch. You can take her back there now, but it won't be safe. *Nowhere* will be safe until we stop it."

"And what information do you think she has?" Avery asked. His voice was cold and tightly controlled.

"I don't know, but *any* information is better than what we have. Just bring her to the infirmary, we can do what we can and find out whatever she knows, and then I'll let you take her back. I swear." I relaxed my grip on his wrist, then deliberately let go of him, dropping my arm to my side.

He stared at me for an uncomfortable moment, and I was inches from losing my temper again when he finally turned and started walking. He didn't say a word, didn't give any indication of his agreement except the fact that he was doing as I'd asked, and not vanishing in a green glow. It was a miracle this guy hadn't already gotten on my last nerve.

The walk to the infirmary was short and silent, full of bare walls and long corridors. I was painfully aware of where the Wall had been; the hall seemed to stretch on forever, and the blank metal surrounding us was empty and accusing. I didn't doubt the tradition of the Wall would start again. One of us would inevitably die, and it was more than likely that those who remembered would continue honoring the dead that way.

It should be Josephine, I thought, unable to help myself. *I should look through her backpack, find something she loved. . . .*

It was a nice thought, but I couldn't bring myself to do it. Not yet. Not when we might soon be nothing but memories.

Avery didn't leave Acacia's side for the next several minutes until she woke. Once he was satisfied that our rudimentary technology would be adequate to help his sister, he stepped back and listened while Jianae (she'd been picked up with Joeb's team, and was one of the few medically trained Walkers we had) asked Acacia questions about her breathing and whether or not she felt dizzy or faint. If I closed my eyes, I could almost pretend I was in a hospital back on my version of Earth.

"She's severely dehydrated and malnourished, but the supplement shots will help with that. The cuts will heal on their own, but I've given her booster pills to make sure they don't get infected," Jianae explained, speaking to both Avery and me. "I can treat the symptoms, but I've never seen this kind of sickness before."

"She's timesick," Avery said quietly. "You can't fix it. TimeWatch can."

I spared him a single glance (Jianae was giving him a similar look as she strapped a pulse monitor to Acacia's wrist), then sat down on the edge of Acacia's bed.

"Hey," I said, not sure where else to start.

She smiled vaguely at me, though her eyes didn't quite focus. It was sort of like she was looking past me, or looking at where I'd been a moment ago. "Hey," she responded, though she paused slightly longer than was normal.

There was another pause, during which I became acutely aware that the last time I'd seen her we'd been inches away from . . . well, I *hoped* it had been about to be a kiss, but there was honestly no way of knowing. I knew she intrigued me, I knew I liked her, and it seemed like she felt the same way. Beyond that . . . it was hard to devote much thought to wondering if I might have a shot with a girl I barely knew when I was supposed to be finding out if the world was about to end.

I sighed. Then I said, "What did you say about Frost-Night and the stars dying?"

"I was worried about you," she said.

"I was worried about you, too," I admitted. "What happened to you?"

She looked briefly irritated. Then she bit her lip and her expression shifted, becoming sad and worried, and—I was surprised to see—scared. "We didn't stop it, Joe."

"I know." I impulsively reached out to take her hand. She didn't react.

"Lord Dogknife . . . threw me out of time," she said, glancing in Avery's direction. "He broke my navigation and shoved me through the dimensions. Through the Nowhere. There was this . . . spider creature. . . ."

I leaned forward, squeezing her hand. Only then did she react, glancing down and giving a faint smile. "Lady Indigo?" I asked. I assumed that was who she meant, but . . .

"You know?"

"I . . ." I started to answer, then paused. I knew what?

"Who?" she asked.

I stared at her. It was starting to sound like we weren't having the same conversation, especially since she wasn't quite making eye contact.

"What?" I asked.

"Did you get hit in the head or something?" she asked.

"No," I said. "Well, I don't think so. Why?"

"What, what?" she asked, beginning to look irritated.

I continued to stare at her, at a loss. "What?"

There was the sudden sound of laughter from behind me, though it was a laugh I didn't recognize. I turned, surprised to find that it was Avery. He was laughing at both of us, his resemblance to Acacia even more obvious in his amusement.

"I really should just let you two talk," he said, still laughing. "But I suppose it would be best if I translate. And, yes," he said, looking at Acacia. "It is."

"What do you mean, translate?"

"Shut up, Avery," Acacia said. "It's not funny."

He grinned at me. I looked between him and Acacia, then blinked. "Did you just . . . ?"

"Respond to her before she spoke? Yes, though not from her point of view. She's timesick," he repeated, some of his good humor fading as he explained. "A side effect of which is time lag. The leader of HEX threw her out of time, as she said. She is not swimming in the same stream, as it were."

"You mean, she's . . . lagging?" I looked back to Acacia, who was glancing between us—but as Avery spoke, she was looking at me.

"Not exactly. She is responding in what she perceives as real time, but her present is not aligned with our present."

"Oh. How can you tell?"

"I'm a Time Agent," he said. "I am trained to see these things."

I fought off a wave of irritation. "I see. So, she was . . ."

"Responding to things you had said a moment before." He grinned at me again. "If the situation weren't so dire, I really would have let it go on. I imagine it would have gotten even funnier."

"Yeah, I'm sure." I glanced back to Acacia, who was looking at Avery. "She wasn't like this when she first showed up, though, was she?"

"It . . . was just starting," Avery explained hesitantly. I

guessed this was more supersecret TimeWatch stuff. "If left unattended, she will continue to slip farther out of this timestream."

"Is that bad?"

He hesitated again. "It is . . . inconvenient. It's danger-ous if allowed to continue for an extended time—months, or years."

I nodded. All that mattered was that it could be fixed, really. I waited until Acacia was looking at me again (and made sure not to move too much, so she could track me) before I spoke. "So if I just . . . go slow, it should be fine . . . ?"

"Yes, if tedious."

"Well, it's a good thing the fate of the Multiverse isn't *urgent* or anything," I snapped. I couldn't help it.

Avery smiled, unruffled. "Yet you were the one who insisted you question her as she is."

I sighed. I waited until Acacia had given her brother a reproachful glance and was looking at me again, then started over.

"Acacia, can you tell me about the stars dying?"

There was another long pause, then her eyes closed and her hand tightened around mine. "The stars and the planets," she said. "FrostNight is moving. It's been moving this whole time . . . but it's not like they meant it to be. It won't sustain itself. It'll die out."

I felt relief go through me so suddenly and strongly that I

felt dizzy. Still, I made myself pause before asking, "It won't sustain itself?"

The allotted time went by before she answered; I was counting roughly six seconds of lag between our exchanges, though I couldn't be sure of how long it took her to process what I was saying and choose her words. "No. I could already feel it dying, but . . . but it's still restarting worlds. I don't know how many already, but it's moving along in a projected arc. . . . Your enemies have already won some new bases," she said, looking away from me. "FrostNight has made empty worlds they can use however they wish."

I squeezed her hand, counted to six, then said, "But this is good, right? We can let it die, concentrate on tracking down that HEX ship and getting it off InterWorld's trail. Right?"

She still wasn't looking at me, even after I counted silently to six. "Acacia? Do you know where it'll end?"

"Yes," she said. "The last projected world is Earth F epsilon ninety-eight to the seventh."

I didn't have to count the six seconds before responding this time. The blood froze in my veins and time actually seemed to slow as I repeated the classification silently to myself. Earth $F\Sigma98^7$. FrostNight had begun on Earth $F\Delta98^6$. The classification of Earths was confusing at best, since there had to be some leeway and margin for error; new Earths were being created all the time and old ones destroyed. The particular subset of Earths in the alpha through omega category were those in the middle of the arc, the ones not inclined strongly toward magic or science. Like mine.

The classification number of my Earth was something I hadn't learned until I'd been on InterWorld for a while; they didn't want to encourage us to be homesick or tempted to go visit. I'd looked up the number on my own, out of curiosity, and I'd always remembered it: Earth $F\Sigma3^{14}$. Earth F epsilon three to the fourteenth.

One of those worlds was mine.

"Joe," Acacia warned, a second before I stood up. Time-sick or not, she apparently hadn't had any trouble reading me. "I know," she said, even as I started to speak.

"That means *my* world will be—" I cut myself off, since she was already nodding.

"I will," Avery said.

"Avery," Acacia said urgently. "You have to tell him."

I looked over at Acacia's brother, picking up on their off-pattern conversation. "Tell me what?"

"That you can't leave," he said.

Screw that. I started for the door.

Avery stepped in front of me, hands held out in front of him. "You must stay here, Harker. There is nothing—"

"Nothing I can do? Screw that," I said, stopping long enough to glare at him. "I can get my family to safety, at the very least."

"And bring them where? Here? To live on InterWorld with

you, the only Walker here to have their loved ones? What of the other Walkers? Some of them may have worlds in the Wave's path, too. Will you give them the same warning?"

"It's only right," I began, but he cut me off.

"And you will all run off into the Multiverse to bring your loved ones into a war they cannot possibly fight. So they will languish on this ship and wait for you—the ones *they* love—to come back from your missions, which some of you inevitably won't."

I glared at him and he matched it, neither of us giving an inch. "Tell me I'm wrong," he demanded.

"You're not. You're not wrong, but what am I supposed to do? Just let my world be destroyed?"

"Worlds die and begin anew every day, Harker, every hour. Yours is nothing special."

I started to push past him, but Acacia (who had probably said this a few seconds ago, according to her) called out, "Listen to him, Joe! TimeWatch can help!"

I stopped, looking at Avery. "How can TimeWatch help?"

"I don't know. I don't know what she's referring to, as it is not our right to interfere with the course of time."

"This has nothing to do with time! It's outside of it, outside of everything, you said so yourself—damn it, you don't have any protocol for this!"

"You're right," he said. "We don't. Which is likely the argument my sister intends to use."

"I don't know," Acacia said, answering my question from a moment ago. "But I can try. And I have to go back anyway. Please, Joe, let me try before you go running off!"

"I will take her back to TimeWatch, get her the care she needs, and discuss this with the council," Avery said. "It will be done as fast as we can possibly make it."

"You're a Time Agent," I shouted, finally losing my temper. All I could think of was the necklace I always wore, the one my mother had made for me the night I'd left home, and how I'd told her I was leaving to protect them. "Time means nothing to you!"

For the first time, I saw him get truly angry. His hand snapped out to clutch my shirt, and I found myself shoved a few steps back.

"Time means *everything* to me," he said, still pressing me backward. "Don't you dare think that because I feel it differently I feel it *less*."

"Is that how you fell in love with Josephine after only five minutes?"

It may have been a cheap shot, but I was pissed off and worried, and I'd been wondering what the hell was up with the two of them ever since he'd called her "Josie."

For a second I thought I was going to get punched, but he let go of me. "Sit down, Acacia," he said, though she hadn't moved yet. Then, to me—"Time flows differently across the worlds, Harker. What was five minutes to you could have been five days to us, or five years. Besides," he finished, a smirk tilting at the corner of his mouth, "where do you think she learned to use a grav-board like that? *You* certainly didn't teach her."

Acacia was getting to her feet anyway, trying to detach all the various wires and monitors she was hooked up to. Jianae was hovering around uncertainly, alternating between helping her unhook herself and telling her she should really stay put.

"Avery, stop," Acacia protested. "Let's just go. Please."

I turned my back on him, going to Acacia. I was seething, furious at Avery and upset by the knowledge that my world was going to die. "Please come back soon, Cay," I told her, and then I reached out to take her face in my hands. "I know this isn't happening for you yet," I said. "But I hope you don't mind when it does." I leaned down and kissed her forehead.

Avery put a hand on Acacia's shoulder, looking disapprovingly at me. "No, I won't tell him," he said, and then they both began to glow green. Acacia smiled at me before they vanished, leaving me to wonder what it was she wanted said.

CHAPTER TEN

"Sir?"

It took me a moment to realize Jianae was addressing me. I was so unused to being addressed like that, like I was in charge, like I was someone who knew what I was doing. Like I was a leader.

Like I was the Old Man.

"It's Joe," I snapped. "And don't look at me like I'm supposed to know what to do."

Her expression changed, becoming sympathetic. "You don't have to know what do," she said, "but you're the only one willing to try so far. Sir."

I stared at her, at this girl I barely even knew, who was telling me I was her leader. It was true, and I knew it; I was the one who'd gathered us all together in the tiniest of hopes that we could somehow stop FrostNight. Not that I knew *how* were supposed to do that . . .

. . . but I had to figure it out. Because I was the only leader they had. Frustrated, I slammed my hand against the wallcom, clicking the link to the engine room. "Jai, are there any extraction teams out currently?"

"I believe Joeb took a team of three out approximately two hours previously."

"Lock us down once they get back. No teams go out again until I say."

"Yes, sir."

"J/O."

"I'm here." His voice came immediately from the speaker. "Is everything—"

"Are the information systems online?"

"I'd kept them shut down to save on power, but I can turn them on again. . . ."

"Do it, and meet me in the library."

"I'm kind of busy driving right now," he said, though his usual snark was missing. He'd been particularly subdued since Avery had brought him back. I was pretty sure I knew why, but that was a problem for another time.

"Our proximity sensors are obviously working, just set the autopilot."

"We actually hit something? I knew the readings said we did, but—"

"Something hit us," I said. "Get to the library and I'll explain everything."

Jai's voice came through the com as I was about to click it off. "Am I to extrapolate from your actions that you have a plan?"

"More or less," I said. "Though it'll probably get a bunch of us killed."

"Better some of us than all of us," he said solemnly, for once speaking plainly.

"Yeah," I agreed. "Something like that."

I'd never been much into reading as a kid—some comics and manga, action stories and the like—but the library at InterWorld had been a refuge of sorts. I'd spent much of what little personal time I'd had sitting in the overstuffed chairs by the fire panel (decorative only, something Jaroux the librarian had insisted on for ambiance) and reading up on the histories of a thousand different worlds. It had been interesting to read about Earths where the Roman Empire had never fallen, where World War II had never happened—or, on some Earths, never ended. There were Earths where Jesus had been female and the great Egyptian emperors had conquered half the world before an asteroid wiped out the other half. It was fascinating, and that's not even counting the histories of the worlds that were nothing like Earth at all.

This was not, of course, the same library—or it was, but far in the future—which turned out to be a blessing, since this InterWorld had had several thousand more years to build up its database.

I sat down near the shattered remains of the fire screen; the chairs were long gone. The words "The place of the cure of the soul" hung faded and smudged on the wall near the ceiling, a nod to the Library at Alexandria, which on some Earths had never burned.

"I need you to access the cataloging system," I told J/O, who was standing over by the info kiosks.

"Okay," he said, reaching out a hand. He inspected the port connection, then flipped one of his fingers back (it always freaked me out when he did that) to reveal a modified mini-USB drive. "What file are you looking for?"

"That is the file," I said. "I don't mean the title index, I mean the files with all the cataloged planets and dimensions."

He hesitated and then reached over to plug himself in. Anyone could use the info kiosk without hooking into it, but J/O's particular body matrix made it easier and faster for him to navigate the system. He could hook his USB finger into the port and traverse it with a thought, not even bothering with voice commands. When we'd been studying together, I'd always found it very unfair that what I had to memorize, he could download straight to his memory banks. That seemed so far away now. We hadn't gotten along at first, but I'd gotten to know him better during our two years training together. He was a lot like me, just . . . younger. He had a lot to prove, and I know he was probably still beating himself up over getting taken over by Binary and trying to kill me.

"I'm taking a chance that you're not still corrupted, you know," I said. He blanched.

"I'm sorry, Joey," he started, but I shook my head.

"It wasn't your fault. You're you again, that's all that matters." I saw a weight visibly lift from him as I spoke. I let that sink in for a moment, then added, "But you should really get some kind of antivirus or something."

"Ha-ha." He made a face, but I could see a small smile tug at the corner of his mouth.

"Seriously, even *my* world has that. Norton or something, y'know?"

"*Fff.* Right. Norton."

We sat in silence for a moment. Though I'd enjoyed teasing him, my thoughts drifted back to Acacia and Avery, and Josephine. Had Avery meant it when he'd said he taught her to use a grav-board? Had they really spent enough time together, in the five minutes it was to me in the Nowhere-at-All, to fall in love? How long had it been for them? I knew that time flowed differently on some worlds. . . . Had he taken her to a place where time moved slower? If he truly had loved her, how had he been able to let her die—no, to strike the killing blow himself? He'd said severing the tie with Lady

Indigo would kill Josephine, yet he'd been willing to do it anyway. Was the alternative horrible enough that killing her had been the only option?

I hadn't liked Avery's attitude from the beginning, but if he'd really spent all that time with Josephine, if he'd brought her back to save us knowing she'd be in danger and then lost her, I supposed I could understand his being less than friendly.

Was that what it would be like for Acacia and me, if we ever got together? Don't get me wrong, I knew I was thinking ahead here. I still barely knew the girl, but there was enough of a *something* between us that I couldn't help putting myself in Josephine's shoes. Had she loved Avery, too? Had she known during those moments they'd spent together that loving a Time Agent was impossible?

J/O interrupted my train of thought. "I think I found it, Joey."

I stood, going to stand behind J/O. A menu with a few different options was visible on the screen, hard to read through the dust and small cracks. It seemed to be what I'd been looking for, but . . . "Can you tell it to dictate?"

"The voice algorithms are corrupted," he said. "The system's been sitting so long that only half of it works."

"Doesn't matter. I want a list of all Earth-classified planets from F delta ninety-eight to the sixth through F epsilon ninety-eight to the seventh."

He paused, clearly recognizing the first classification. I wasn't surprised. It was the Binary world he'd been corrupted on, where we'd first retrieved Joaquim, the Walker who'd turned out to not be a Walker at all. . . .

Frankly speaking, it was the world where everything had first gone to hell in the proverbial handbasket.

"Okay," J/O said. "It's indexing." He paused again, obviously scanning the results. "It's . . . that's a lot of planets, Joey."

"I know."

"What am I looking for?"

"Just project the list for me."

He looked around to find a flat surface, finally settling on the wall to my left. His cybernetic eye grew brighter, the little circuits visible in the iris flaring to life. A blank square appeared on the wall, like when a projector first turns on before the movie starts, then words started to appear and scroll like the end credits, almost faster than I could read.

Earth FΔ98^6

Earth FΔ98$^6_{+1}$

Earth FΔ98$^6_{+2}$

Earth FΔ98$^6_{+3}$

Earth FΔ98$^6_{+4}$

Earth FΔ98$^6_{+5}$

"Go ahead and collapse subcategories," I said quickly.

"One moment." The classifications vanished, then started again.

Earth FΔ98^6

Earth FΔ98^5

Earth FΔ98^4

Earth FΔ98^3

Earth FΔ98^2

Earth FΔ98^1

Earth FΔ99

It went on for a while. There were a lot of different Earths (an infinite number, actually, since they were being destroyed and created every second, even *without* FrostNight roaming the Multiverse like a gleeful lawn mower), and it's not like I was looking for one in specific. The problem with the Multiverse was that planets and dimensions existed all over the place; classifying and numbering them in a linear way was almost impossible. The basic idea was that the letters (mostly) ran up and down, while the numbers (mostly) ran side to side. Just knowing where FrostNight's path of destruction started and where it ended wasn't enough, since it could take any number of different roads to get there. My world was close enough to the end that I knew FrostNight would eventually wipe out that entire classification; I was just trying to figure out how it was getting there so I could have a chance at stopping it.

I was in the middle of figuring out how to find the most likely projected path when the numbers suddenly dimmed. I glanced over to J/O, trying to make sure he wasn't losing power or something, but he looked as confused as I did.

"Joey, there's a—"

More words flashed up on the wall.

OFFICER CLEARANCE GRANTED.

"J/O, how did you—"

"I'm not doing it," he said. "It's a programmed variable; it's reacting to the search parameters from this location and some other factors."

"What other factors?" I asked, but the words flashed and faded, and an image appeared on the wall.

It was faint and fuzzy, grainy, like old silent movies from the nineteen twenties. It took me a moment to even place what the image was supposed to be, but humans are trained to recognize faces first—and one face you'll always recognize is your own, even if it is a few decades older and sporting an artificial eye.

It was the Old Man. Captain Joseph Harker, leader of InterWorld.

He was sitting behind his desk, looking seriously at whatever was recording this message. He started to speak, his mouth obviously moving, though the graininess of the video made it difficult to read his lips.

"J/O, the sound!"

"What am I, a home theater system? You want some popcorn, too?"

"J/O—"

"I'm trying, Joey. This file is *really* old."

I glued my eyes to the image, trying to catch whatever I could of what he was saying. I almost jumped out of my skin as, a moment later, J/O started to talk in the Old Man's voice.

"—to give you a few moments to sort out this file, since I don't know exactly how old it will be by the time you see it. Once you have everything in order, give the voice command 'proceed,' or select 'continue' on whatever kiosk you're at. I'll wait."

The way he said "I'll wait" simultaneously made me smile and hurry the hell up; it was the same impatient tone he always used, the one that meant *I'll wait, but you'd better make this* fast, *before I lose my patience.*

"Proceed?"

"Voice recognition's broken, Joey, I told you that," J/O said in his own voice. I glanced over to the kiosk, where the word "continue" was visible among the cracks in the screen. I tapped a finger to it, then two fingers. Then, when still nothing happened, I hit it with the side of my fist. The screen flashed.

"Very well," said J/O in the Old Man's voice, as the projection started speaking once again. "Joseph Harker of Earth F epsilon three to the fourteenth, I trust it is you receiving this message."

"Yes," I said automatically, even though I knew he couldn't hear me. It was just a recording. A recording that the

Old Man had programmed specifically for *me*, one that had been floating around in InterWorld's database for thousands of years.

"Though I am unaware of your precise situation at the time of this recording, I am certain of two things. One, that you are currently on a future version of this ship, and two, that InterWorld Prime is doomed." He looked straight at me, and I swear it was almost like we were locking gazes, like he knew exactly where I was standing in the room.

"The HEX ship *Adraedan* has a lock on us, and I've thrown the engines into overdrive. We can't outrun them, and we can't out-Walk them. They're keeping pace with our dimensional shifts, and if we stop even for a moment, they'll have us.

"That being said, you seeing this message means I have three things to tell you." He held up one finger. "One. I had Jaroux set certain protocols in place to alert me when this message was received. I have the precise date; binary time stamp; and, thanks to the tracer I injected you with last week, your exact location." Before I could react to *that* (that stupid tracer had come into play more times than a golygon has right angles), he dropped another bomb on me.

"I have likely just given the order to evacuate InterWorld Prime entirely, which means the remaining Walkers on this ship will be coming to you any second now. I hope you have the port room ready."

I ran to the com system on the nearest wall, jabbing my finger at the main broadcast link. "Jai, ready the port room, we have incoming Walkers!" I yelled.

"Two," the Old Man was saying, holding up two fingers now. I stared up at the projection, skewed and larger than life now that I was standing beneath it. "Try to keep Hue with you at all times. He'll be more useful than you know."

My stomach sank down to the floor as I listened. He was giving me advice like he wasn't going to see me, to Walk over with the rest coming from InterWorld Prime. He wasn't coming. . . . Why would he not come?

"Three." He dropped his hand altogether, looking at me seriously. The barest hint of a smile ghosted across his face, just for a moment. "It is impossible," he said. "Do it anyway. It's worth it." I had no idea what he was talking about, until he added, "She liked orange roses, when I knew her."

With no further warning, the image blinked out.

"J/O," I said, before he could say anything, "get to the port room and help Jai, *now.*"

He spared a single glance back to the wall where the projection had been, then darted off. I jammed my fingers against the com again. "Jai, J/O's coming to help."

"They're here, sir," Jai's voice came back over the com. "They're all here."

"What about the Old Man? Is Captain Harker with them?"

"He stayed." Another voice came over the com. After a moment I recognized Jaroux's calm, smooth tones. "None of us knew he was going to, but he stayed. I think you know why."

I let my arm fall to my side, gaze drifting to the wall where the projection had been. "Damn you," I told it. "God damn you."

"Sir?" Jai's voice echoed through the speakers. "What now?"

After a moment, I lifted my hand to the speaker again. "Get everyone organized," I said. "Make sure anyone who needs to eat or sleep can do that, and send any injured to the infirmary."

"Yes, sir," said Jai. "Should our recent arrivals expect your appearance at this juncture?"

"No." I paused, double-checking myself, surprised by the calm certainty that had suddenly come over me. There was one thing I could do, and I had to do it. I knew I had to. "Jai, J/O, and Jo, you're in charge. I'm stepping out for a moment. I'll be back with the Old Man."

There was a moment of silence over the com, and I shut it off before the flurry of protests could begin. The ship was up and running again, which meant we'd realigned with our own timestream, which meant we didn't need Hue to Walk. InterWorld Beta had its own formula now, which Joeb had been using for the past two days to Walk back and forth with new recruits. I didn't have to travel through time to get where I needed to go. I could Walk, like I always did, sideways through the dimensions.

The other point was that the Old Man had stopped running to let everyone off. That meant the ship wasn't moving anymore, wasn't locked in a perpetual warp—which meant my old InterWorld Prime formula should work again.

The thing about the InterWorld address was that it always stayed the same, no matter where the ship was. It was static, constant, unchanging—but the ship had to actually *be* static for the address to work. It hadn't been for the past few days. Now it was, and I could Walk there on my own.

I closed my eyes and drew in a breath, calling the old InterWorld formula to mind. It burned in my head like a beacon, like a North Star, like a lighthouse.

$\{IW\}:=\Omega/\infty$

I saw the path open up before me, and I—

—found myself flat on my back as something hurtled into me, the texture of it like a combination between glossy tissue paper and a rubber band. I opened my eyes to find Hue hovering above me, flashing various colors of *concerned*.

"Hue . . . ! What are you doing?" The last time I'd seen him, he'd been sleeping (or what appeared to be sleeping, anyway) in my quarters, tired out from all the TimeWalking he'd been helping us do. Joeb had taken him out a few times to help with getting Walkers, and the poor thing had been exhausted. Not only that, but I think Josephine's death had actually hit him pretty hard. They hadn't interacted that much, what with Josephine having shot at him once and all, but I was fairly certain he still understood death and missed her. It was sometimes hard to figure how much he *did* understand, but he tended to grasp most concepts and things I asked him to do, and seemed to have his own opinions on situations.

Like now, for example.

I sat up, trying to get to my feet. Hue floated around me, bobbing back and forth. "What's wrong with you?" I asked. "Why did you stop me?"

He flickered a few different colors, then turned black, little red flashes crawling over his surface like lightning. I wasn't sure exactly what he was trying to say, but it definitely looked foreboding.

"I have to go, Hue," I tried. "I have to help the Old Man."

His color faded from the top down, something that usually meant *no.*

"Yes, I do. I have to try."

This time he brightened, which confused me. He agreed that I had to try, but he wouldn't let me go?

Confused or not, it wasn't like I hadn't played this game before. I knew my mudluff friend pretty well, and we'd worked out a pretty accurate system of communication.

"I have to try, but you won't let me go?" I asked.

He turned an agitated shade of purple, floating forward. He shifted colors a bit, making a dark spot in his center, with lines of blue circuits moving out from it. He looked like a giant eye—like the Old Man's binary eye.

"The Old Man?" I asked. He brightened. "What about him?"

This time he turned blue and green, with little patches of white. The colors reminded me of home. "Earth?"

He brightened.

I didn't know what to say to that. How could he possibly be on Earth somewhere? And *which* Earth?

"Can you take me to him?"

Hue hesitated. He flickered uncertainly, a few random numbers and equations moving across his surface. It was the first time I'd seen him use anything other than colors to communicate, but I wasn't sure what he was trying to say.

"Look, just do it," I said, frustrated. Hue seemed to be implying that the Old Man was moving around freely, that he wasn't a prisoner of HEX as I had thought, but I was still worried about him. I needed to find him, and Hue had never steered me wrong before. Plus, the Old Man's message had said to keep him with me. . . . "Do it however you think is best, but help me find the Old Man. Please."

He seemed to sigh, a faint gray washing over his spherical body. Then, with no warning at all, he launched himself at me.

I didn't panic, mostly because he'd done this kind of thing

before. In fact, he'd done this exact thing before, when he'd once rescued me from HEX. We collided and I felt his presence in the back of my mind, faint and intangible. Together, we Walked.

The place between dimensions was known to us as the In-Between; I know I've mentioned it before. What I haven't really done is explain it, and that's partially because it's more than a little hard to explain. The In-Between is like looking through a kaleidoscope that shows you images from a hundred other kaleidoscopes, all of which have pictures of things instead of colors and shapes. There are also thousands, if not millions, of sounds and smells and textures. There are legends about Walkers going insane after their first trip through, and I was more than willing to believe those stories were real.

The benefit of going through it with Hue, though, was that the In-Between is a multidimensional place—and as a multidimensional creature, Hue was a local. When I looked through my eyes with Hue in the back of my head acting as a perception filter, all the chaos of the In-Between made perfect sense.

I stood on what looked like a pile of discarded paper cups, though they were all fused together and felt like a trampoline beneath my feet. I looked off into the distance, ignoring the flock of origami birds, the sudden smell of fried eggs, and the abrupt understanding of the color blue. I expanded my senses and looked with more than my eyes.

I was aware of InterWorld, the beautiful bubble-dome city I'd called my home for the past two years. It felt like when you put drops of food coloring into clear water, how the color slowly permeates the liquid. InterWorld was the water, and the ink was HEX.

I wrenched my mind away from that knowledge, focusing instead on the Old Man.

And I found him.

The equation came immediately to mind: Earth $F\Sigma 3^{14}$. My world.

And beyond it was . . . nothing. The organized chaos of the In-Between stretched into pure, oppressive *nothing*, the complete absence of everything and anything. It wasn't even a void, it was more complete than that. More final.

It was a world on the edge of a precipice, an abyss, a yawning chasm of infinite nothingness. A world clinging tightly to its universe, still turning, holding on to the end.

I focused on the Old Man, on that world, on the edge of nothing. And I Walked as fast as I could.

There were hundreds of portals to Walk through in my town alone, but the one I was most familiar with was the one in the park. It wasn't always in the same place, but it had been there every time I'd needed it.

This park was where I'd first been captured by HEX, before I'd ever been to InterWorld. It was where I'd landed when Lord Dogknife had thrown me through the dimensions. It was where I'd said a final farewell to my world a few short days ago, and it was where I landed now.

It was the middle of the afternoon. There were families picnicking, children climbing on the modestly sized play set, people walking their dogs and playing catch and throwing Frisbees. There were birds chirping. And somewhere, nearby, was the Old Man.

I could sense him. I could sense him here, and I could sense the ever-present *nothing* looming on the horizon.

I bolted through the park, not caring if anyone saw me. I ran past a couple out for a stroll, a man pushing a double-wide stroller, and a woman strutting down the street on heels that could probably be used as a weapon. I dodged through a group of kids playing tag, ignoring the faint twinge in my ribs as my foot came down hard in a dip in the ground, jarring my entire body.

Within moments, I was across the street and running down the same sidewalks I used to ride my bike on every day after school. The kid next door, twentysomething now and home from college, was riding his skateboard directly toward me. "Hey—" he started, recognizing me as I jumped off the sidewalk, running down the middle of the street. The dotted yellow lines moved beneath me, one by one. The sky seemed darker than it had a moment ago. A shadow was moving across the sun.

Time seemed to slow down as I rounded the corner onto my street. The wind blew dried leaves between my feet as I ran, and the red brake lights of my family's van winked out as they finished pulling into the driveway.

Blue, silver, green, gray, black. Hue was communicating silent panic in the back of my mind, but I still didn't speak his language.

My dad was lifting two bags of groceries out of the trunk. Mom was unbuckling the Squid from his car seat and settling him on her hip, helping him readjust his grip on the little container of bubble solution they'd probably just bought him at the store. Jenny was pulling her backpack out of the car, laughing at something our dad had said, and standing in the shade of the rickety old tree house I'd hardly ever played in was the Old Man.

My family didn't see him. Mom turned to say something to Dad as he started to take the groceries inside, and I swear she must have looked right at the Old Man, but she didn't see him at all. Mom and Dad were smiling at each other, and the Old Man was watching. He was smiling, too.

He was standing in the grass, just standing, arms dangling at his sides. He looked peaceful, like this was all he'd ever wanted. Like he'd been waiting for this moment his entire life.

"Mom, Dad!!" I shouted, but the wind stole my words away. It was a blue wind, a silver wind, and it was blowing so fast it was getting hard to see. It was stealing the colors, draining the green from the grass and turning everything to gray. It blew the bark right off the trees, the texture off the buildings, and every speck of sand and rock came pixel by pixel off the asphalt.

They all swirled around me, becoming numbers and letters and equations as they passed. Everything was dissolving into data around us, and he was still smiling. They were swirling around him, too, and then some of them spun off. They created a mini dust devil in front of him, moving counter to the rest of the whirlwind, forming into the shape of a woman. She raised a hand comprised entirely of elements from the periodic table, and all the swirling figures sparked green. She moved her fingers around like writing, and then the wind changed, moving in the opposite direction. Counterclockwise, now.

She leaned down to kiss him with elliptic lips, the logarithmic spirals of her hair whipping around the perfect numbers of her face. Then the pixels and symbols and sums and products flying up from the world around me all connected, humming and buzzing like a swarm of bees. They swirled around me, obscuring my vision of the Old Man and the woman made of figures. They attached themselves to me like metal to a magnet, and I knew no more.

CHAPTER ELEVEN

I'M SORRY.

I couldn't stop it. I can't stop it. I don't even know if I want to. Isn't this my destiny?

"The pup awakes."

"You were informed of his condition already. You were told he would wake."

"I still don't understand your decision to bring him here. It was my wish that he be erased along with his world."

"Your passion is your folly. It would be a logical waste for the Harker to die when we can still use him, especially since your plan to entrap the other Walkers has failed."

There was a sound like the snarling of an animal: a low, warning, guttural growl. "Your *science* has failed us as well, has it not? FrostNight is not strong enough to perpetuate itself."

"Which is why we can still use the Harker."

"He has escaped us twice now," the first voice snarled. I was all too aware of who it was—it was the *only* thing I was aware of, right now. Lord Dogknife.

My brain felt like it was swirling around inside my head, and it kept repeating words I couldn't attribute a voice to: *I can't stop it.*

"And the last time," the voice went on, "it was *my* perseverance that kept him and the girl from interfering with the *Adraedan*'s lock on InterWorld."

"A plan which ultimately failed."

"That matters little, as we have found the power from another source. We can perpetuate the Wave even without the Harker."

"Yet your other power source is not as strong. With the Harker, we are guaranteed success. It is the clear choice."

They continued to argue, but the voices faded into the background. I didn't care what they were saying. I didn't care where I was, or what was going to happen to me.

My world was dead.

My family was dead. My supportive, good-natured father who always stood up for what was right and my smart, creative mother who'd not only believed my crazy tale about being an interdimensional freedom fighter, she'd made me a necklace and wished me good luck and let me leave home forever. My funny, sensitive little sister and my adorable baby brother who loved Cheerios and blowing bubbles. Mr. Dimas. The boy riding his skateboard down the street, and the nice lady next door who'd babysat for me sometimes when I was younger. They were all gone.

And the Old Man had stood there and watched it happen. He'd stood there and *smiled*.

We'd trusted him. We'd *all* trusted him, we'd all been willing to die for him if necessary. We all knew why we were on InterWorld, why we'd been chosen, what we were doing. We'd all taken the oath and knew the risks.

And in the end, he'd dumped everyone onto a half-working ship, abandoned our Prime ship—our *home*—to HEX, and watched the destruction of my world without doing a thing to stop it.

I opened my eyes.

I had a headache like nothing I'd ever felt before, and I could vaguely feel Hue in the back of my mind. As I had been when FrostNight was first released, I was captive on what looked to be a Binary world. Everything was shiny and smooth, all angles and clean glass. I wasn't in the same kind of mesh cage I'd woken up in before, but I was still bound. I was lying on the floor, pale wires snaking around me. I knew they would be laid out in a five-pointed star, likely inverted, before I even looked. I also knew I was at the center of it.

My hands were bound, each wrist held to the floor by about a foot of thick white chain. They were made of something lighter than metal, but it seemed a lot sturdier. The floor was white tile, so bright it hurt my eyes to look at. There was a single spire standing at each point of the circuitry star, five in total, with a small globe at the top of each. They looked like conductors, or something similar.

"Good morning, pup."

Lord Dogknife's growling voice was unmistakable, and the leader of HEX looked at me with distaste, lip curling back as though he didn't like the scent of me. Lord Dogknife was taller than anyone I'd known on my world, powerful and perfectly muscled. The word "Adonis" came to mind, pretty much at the same time as "Anubis," which was an equally apt description. He had a head like a wolf or hyena, though it still somehow bore a strong resemblance to a human face. It was like he'd gotten stuck halfway through transforming.

I ignored him. I forced myself into a sitting position and looked around, dully curious as to the rest of my surroundings. There was a sharp ache in my chest, like my heart had turned to ice and shattered. It hurt to breathe, to think, to even *be*. My world was gone. What was I fighting for now?

"I suppose I should thank you for one thing, at least," Lord Dogknife said. I continued to ignore him, though there was this strange *tick-tick-tick* sound that filled me with an unidentifiable dread. I looked back, trying to find the source of it—and there, approaching on Lord Dogknife's right, was Lady Indigo.

She was still a giant spider thing, her bonelike append-ages being used as legs now rather than wings. Her skin was still reddish and transparent, her bones visible beneath her rubbery flesh.

"You've returned one of my generals to me," Lord Dog-knife said with a smile, reaching out to run his hand along one of the long bones that arced up from her back. She was using them to walk, like a spider, though her body was verti-cal instead of horizontal, her feet not touching the ground. "And now, since you're here, I can keep her."

Ah. Lady Indigo was the alternate power source Lord Dogknife had mentioned. I supposed that made sense, con-sidering the power she had from the things she'd absorbed in the Nowhere-at-All. . . . "Hello again, Harker," she said. I could barely hear her over the memories of my comrades screaming as she absorbed their essences.

"I almost thought you were going to invite me to your lovely home when last we met," she said, her lips peeling back over her teeth in a horrific grin. "Tell me, how did you man-age to break my link with your tasty friend?"

I swallowed thickly, remembering Josephine's last moments, the way she and Avery had smiled at each other before he sliced through the threads around her with his cir-cuitry sword. I remembered the way she'd taken InterWorld's oath before she died.

They watched me for a moment; when I didn't respond,

Lord Dogknife gave her a soothing smile. "It hardly matters, Lady Indigo. In mere moments, everything will be ours."

She smiled again, pleased. "I know you wished him dead on his world, Lord Dogknife, but I must say I agree with the Professor's decision to bring him here. This way is so much better. The InterWorld ship is still so full of tasssssty Walkers. . . ."

"Once FrostNight is fully powered, the Walkers will be of no more concern to us," Lord Dogknife reminded her. "Our ascension will ensure that."

Lady Indigo frowned. "But the InterWorld vessel will be one of the last—"

"Hush, my dear," he said, though there was an undercurrent of a growl to it once again. "The Harker is clever. We mustn't say too much."

"The Harker isssssss . . . clever. . . ." she repeated, looking at me hungrily. Literally hungrily, like she wanted to eat me.

"FrostNight will be upon us soon. It will return to its roost, and we will feed it as mother birds."

"Mother . . . mother birdssssss . . ."

I looked away, still only partially able to summon up any measure of caring. The only thing that piqued my interest at all was Lord Dogknife's warning to not say anything more in front of me. I was the thorn in his paw, and he was starting to recognize it. I smiled grimly. That was fitting. That was all InterWorld had ever been able to be.

InterWorld will be one of the last, she'd said. I supposed that was a small comfort, but when FrostNight came, it would wipe out everything. Like it had wiped out my planet.

That sharp, stabbing ache made itself known in my chest again, and I ignored the little voice in my head that whispered *fight*. What would I fight for? Revenge? That was useless.

There was a huge computer on the far wall, seamless and white, and a full screen with programs opening and closing in rapid succession. I knew without even a second thought that this was the Professor's nonhuman form. It seemed to be controlling all the power in the area; the programs on the monitor seemed to correspond with bits of equipment all over the room powering on or off.

I concentrated, somewhat listlessly casting about for a portal. I thought I sensed the mere thread of one, somewhere close, but I couldn't reach it. The chains kept me from Walking, which I had more or less expected. I was able to pick up on the classification for this planet, though; Earth $F\epsilon 98^7$. The last projected planet in FrostNight's path.

"FrostNight comes," said Lord Dogknife. I was getting really tired of hearing those words.

This was it. FrostNight would come here, would drain me of everything that made me *me*, as it had nearly done before. Then it would go on to reshape the Multiverse.

My earlier apathy faded a bit at the thought. Yes, *my* world was dead, but there were an infinite number of other worlds.

There were an infinite number of my para-incarnations yet to be discovered, and all of them had parents. I couldn't save *my* mother and father, but mine weren't the only ones out there.

And beyond that, what about my comrades, waiting on InterWorld Beta? I had told them I would be back with the Old Man. Who would they look to now that he was dead?

I suspected I knew the answer, but I didn't like it any. They'd look to me, if I made it out of here alive.

Lady Indigo had said InterWorld would be the last, or one of the last. I assumed she meant the last thing left; I didn't know for certain, but it seemed like an educated guess. Lord Dogknife had said they would "ascend." What did *that* mean? FrostNight had to *stop* at some point, right? If it was going to reshape the Multiverse, there had to be a point where it would accomplish its goal and cease to be, right? Maybe if InterWorld went into a perpetual warp again, or something . . . maybe they could outrun it.

That was doubtful; Acacia had said she could run any-where in the Multiverse, and she didn't think there was anywhere that would be safe. If not even TimeWatch (and I had no idea where TimeWatch actually *was*, it just seemed likely that an organization existing for the sole purpose of protecting time would be pretty remote) would be safe, I couldn't imagine InterWorld being able to outrun FrostNight.

Still, it was the only chance they had. Maybe if I could send Hue to them, tell them to warp . . . It was either that, or hope that TimeWatch would somehow come in and save the day.

As before, Hue was a dim presence in the back of my mind. He did that sometimes, seeming to sort of merge with me without giving me all the crazy vision-into-time-and-space stuff.

Hue, I thought, not sure if he'd be able to hear me at all. *Hue, are you there?*

I got the brief impression of a contracting pupil, or a deflating balloon, along with the connotation of *fear*.

I know, buddy. Me, too. I know you tried to warn me back there. You can go, okay? You can go where it might be safer, you just have to warn the others.

Not that I knew *how* he was going to warn them. Even I had trouble communicating with Hue, and I knew him better than any of the other Walkers.

"Sssssso sad . . . the Harker won't speak. He dislikessss usss. . . ."

Lady Indigo's voice drew my attention to her and Lord Dogknife. They were standing together at one of the pillars, watching me intently. They were watching me so intently that neither of them noticed the faint green glow sparking in the air behind them, like a lighthouse through a distant storm.

"'Dislike' is a pretty mild word for it," I told her, feeling a smile curl at the corners of my mouth. "'Hate' would be closer. But you know what?"

She tilted her head to an angle that didn't look possible, let alone comfortable.

"I don't hate you nearly as much as *he* does."

Her face registered confusion for a brief moment—then pain, as Avery's circuitry blade cut through the air and sliced into one of the bones holding her up.

She screamed, staggering sideways as the limb buckled beneath her and the others shifted to compensate. She skittered around to face the dark-haired, violet-eyed boy, standing with sword at the ready.

"Hello, lovely," he said. "I think we're overdue for a conversation."

She snarled, swiping at him with one of her limbs. It was long and razor sharp at the end, but Avery moved so fast he seemed to blur, slicing his sword out at the same time. Lord Dogknife moved as well, lifting a hand in preparation for some kind of spell.

"Avery, watch out!" I called, at the same time a bolt of dark-looking energy was loosed from Lord Dogknife's palm. Avery brought his sword up once again, deflecting whatever it had been, and then there was another green glow sparking through the air right in front of me.

"Hey, Joe," Acacia whispered, appearing so close to me I felt her breath on my face. "Let's get you out of here."

I swallowed, suddenly unable to form words. Emotions

and thoughts went rapidly through my mind. Relief first, relief that I wasn't here alone anymore, that they had come to my rescue. Apathy again, because I wanted to tell her what had happened to my world but didn't have the words, and finally anger. Anger, because she had said TimeWatch would help. She had made me let her go and she'd left me with the promise that she would do something to save my world, and she hadn't.

"You're a little late," I said, unable to keep the edge from my voice.

She didn't even glance up at me as she put both hands on the thick white chains that held me to the floor. "Not now, Joe." The sounds of battle could be heard around us, as Avery continued to dodge Lady Indigo and deflect the magic from Lord Dogknife. "He can't hold them off for long. We've got to get you out of here."

"Why?" I watched her fingernails glow green on both hands, the little circuits pulsing with energy. "So we can all go back to InterWorld and pick up the pieces like some big, happy family?"

"Don't do the bitter self-pity thing, Joe, it really doesn't suit you."

I glanced away, stung—in time to see Lord Dogknife, bleeding from a gash on his snout, turn and fire another bolt of energy toward us.

"Acacia!" Avery and I shouted out a warning at the same

time, but the bolt crashed into her before she had time to move. She was knocked a few yards away from me, though she tucked and rolled to come up in a defensive crouch. Little lines of electricity crawled over her for a moment like the remnants of a static shock, and I remembered her using some kind of skin shield before. She seemed unhurt, which was good; it meant she was able to dodge the next thing Lord Dogknife sent at her, which looked like a flurry of bats with vapory, red bodies.

I focused inward again, intending to convince Hue to go tell InterWorld to punch it. When there was no response, I realized he was completely gone from my mind. I hadn't even noticed him leave.

Good luck, little buddy, I thought, as I saw at least two doors on opposite sides of the room slide open, and the glassy-eyed clones Binary used as their grunt army started to pour through. The cavalry was here, and it wasn't on our side.

Then a feeling as familiar to me as my own heartbeat tingled in the air, like a scent you've known your whole life coming to you on a sudden breeze. Lady Indigo whipped her head up in obvious joy, letting loose a wild howl.

"They come! Like moths to a flame, they come!"

And just like that, the room was filled with Walkers. I had no idea how they'd all gotten through the same portal—and then I saw Hue, bobbing above Jai's head. He must have somehow expanded the gateway.

"To the Captain!" Joeb cried. I flinched.

The room burst into a flurry of motion. The huge screen on the far wall—the Professor, leader of Binary—flared to life once again, and so did the white cables that made up the star I was in the center of. The first Walker to me, someone I didn't even recognize, tried to cross over one of the cables and was launched backward. The others slowed, one kneeling to check on our fallen comrade, the rest either breaking off to deal with the Binary clones or trying to find some way to bypass the wires.

J/O stopped at the edge of the star, talking to Jai, and I realized I couldn't hear them. When the wires had flared to life, a shimmery, barely visible shield had sprung up around the edges of the star. It fed upward into the conductors and continued into the ceiling. Abruptly, I felt like I was in some kind of vacuum. I couldn't hear a thing happening beyond it.

It was surreal, like watching an action movie on mute. Everything was chaos beyond the translucent walls, but I heard nothing.

Acacia was trading blows with Lord Dogknife, dodging and weaving around the various bits of equipment and Walkers, alternately shielding herself and firing various weapons and gadgets from her tool belt. She looked to be holding her own; unfortunately, so did Lord Dogknife.

Avery was doing much the same with Lady Indigo, now wielding the sword in one hand and what looked like a long tube in the other. As he brought the tube up to block one of the razor-sharp bones Lady Indigo was using as weapons, I realized it was his scabbard.

Lady Indigo wasn't doing as well as Lord Dogknife seemed to be. Of her eight bonelike legs, two had been sliced cleanly off at the joints, and one was tucked up, wounded and useless, near her body. Still arguably less than sane, she was laughing and cackling at the Time Agent even as he cut close enough to sever a few strands of what hair remained on her head.

The air was full of projectiles going back and forth between the Walkers and the clones, in some places flying so thickly I could hardly see. This wasn't the entire base—that would have been nearly five hundred or so of us, and though the room was big enough to fit that many, there seemed to be about half that number here now. But the others were here, too—I could sense them, outside this room, keeping more of the clones from getting in.

They had come for me. Every single one of them, even the injured. Every Walker on Base Town had come here, to the end of the Multiverse, for me.

I glanced down at the chains Acacia had been working on, giving them an experimental tug; one of the links looked transparent, which I was hoping meant it was damaged. I wrapped it around my wrist (the broken one, of course . . .) to get better leverage, and pulled with all my might.

I looked around as I strained, using what I saw as both distraction and encouragement. Jo was helping Acacia, flying around and taking shots at Lord Dogknife with a blaster she'd picked up from one of the Binary clones. J/O and Jai had both run over to the Professor himself and seemed to be having a heated argument, while some of the other Walkers—I recognized Josef and Jakon in particular—fought to protect them from the live wires that snapped through the air like whips.

I felt the searing pain in my wrist at the same time I felt the chain come loose, and my own momentum sent me toppling over to one side. I had one hand free, though, and that meant I could use both hands to pull the other chain off.

I wrapped the chain around both hands and pulled again, bracing my feet against where it attached to the floor. After a long moment I had to give in, panting and sweating from the effort. It hadn't even budged. Acacia hadn't managed to damage this one. I had nothing on me but Josephine's switchblade; it was a good knife, the blade about two and a half inches, the handle sturdy. Still, I didn't think it would do much to damage these chains.

I looked around again. Hue was bobbing anxiously around the outside of the star, pulsing different shades of blue and silver. J/O and Jai were still arguing. Finally, J/O shouted something at Jai, who hung his head and nodded. As one, they turned and dodged through the mass of writhing, tentacle-like wires, moving right up to the giant machine. J/O flipped one of his fingers back to reveal the mini-USB, and Jai put both hands on either side of the cyborg's head.

"NO!" I screamed, uselessly—they couldn't hear me. Jai's whole body glowed red. So did J/O, as the younger incarnation of me plugged the USB into one of the many panels on the giant machine.

There was a sound like the screeching of metal, something even I could hear. It seemed to be coming from the very walls, from every bit of equipment in the room, and from the wires that surrounded me.

The transparent walls caging me dropped. At the same time, every single Binary clone in the room froze, some of them dropping to the floor. Over by the sparking, smoking machine that had housed Binary's leader, J/O and Jai did as well.

Josef charged over to me, pulling at the chain with one massive hand. As he broke the remaining link, he grabbed me with his other hand, tucking me up under his arm like a football. Hue whirled around us, those strange equations flickering across his surface again, like he'd done back in the library.

"Get him out of here!" Acacia screamed, but I expertly wriggled free of Josef's huge grasp. "Joe, *go!*"

I ignored her, running over to Jai and J/O. With a quick glance, I could see that Jai was breathing shallowly. The massive machine against the wall was still sparking, emitting a sickly red smoke. J/O was doing the same.

I pulled the cyborg to me, starting to check various different vitals and finding all of them useless. He was half robot, he had very few of the human life signals. I coughed, waving the smoke away, and passed a hand in front of his eyes. There was no reaction.

One of his eyes, like mine, was brown. The other was red, like it was sometimes when he was using it to project an image or searching internal memory banks. But this time it was different. It was a dull red, with a small black dot in the center. It looked like a powered-off machine. Lifeless.

Out of everyone at InterWorld, J/O looked the most like me. He looked like a younger me, and it was beyond awful to sit there and look at my face with no life in it.

It wasn't the first time I'd had to do that. I also knew it wouldn't be the last.

I looked up. The Binary clones that hadn't fallen were moving again; there were fewer of them by about half, but they still outnumbered us. J/O and Jai might have managed to destroy the Professor's mechanical vessel, but he had to exist elsewhere as well.

Right as that thought went through my mind, one of the clones near me shifted into the figure I remembered, with the unwrinkled pants and tweed jacket and bow tie. He still wore the Coke-bottle glasses, but one of the lenses was cracked and his hair was mussed. His eyes still contained nothing but static, and I could still tell he was looking at me.

"Very clever," he said emotionlessly. "But an ultimately useless sacrifice. Our Silver Dream awakens. The Wave is coming."

As before, it was like a shadow was passing over the sun. The room darkened, and I got the impression that the colors were all whipping away on the sudden wind.

"Joe!" Acacia screamed. "Get—" Whatever else she was saying was cut off. There was a sudden sound like rolling thunder, deafening and ominous, and a dark flash. Avery yelled incoherently, and through the mass combat of Walkers and Binary scouts, I caught a glimpse of Acacia curled up in a crumpled heap on the floor. There was some kind of dark rune circle pulsing a sickly purple beneath her. Avery slashed at Lady Indigo with his sword, trying to dodge around to get to his sister, but she wheeled and caught him with one of her legs, knocking him into the far wall.

I started forward, but a sudden flare of dark mist rose up in front of me, and a strong hand grabbed me by the throat.

I felt my feet leave the ground as Lord Dogknife raised me to his eye level, black fog rising up off his skin like steam on a summer day. His breath smelled like carrion, and I felt a wave of nausea sweep over me as he growled in my face.

"You have been nothing but a thorn in my side since we

met, little Harker," he hissed, shaking me like a misbehaving pup.

I couldn't help it; I laughed. He'd used almost the exact same phrasing I'd thought to myself, and for some reason in that moment, it was funny.

His red eyes narrowed to slits as he looked at me. What little peripheral vision I had told me my friends were trying to get to us, but most of them had their own problems; there were still several hundred Binary clones firing plasma blobs and wielding electroneural emitters to deal with. Hue was hovering nearby, alternating various colors of *distressed*, but he couldn't help, either.

"You find something amusing, little Walker?" he hissed. "I would adorn my throne with your skin, were you not going directly into the heart of FrostNight himself. Do you see, little Walker? He comes for you."

The equations were dancing in the air again, numbers and letters and formulas, and I struggled against Lord Dogknife's grip. I couldn't see Avery or Acacia from here, but I could still hear Lady Indigo cackling. I didn't have any kind of weapon on me at all, and FrostNight was swirling all around, ready to destroy this world with me on it, to feed off me. . . .

Then, abruptly, it all constricted. All the numbers and letters and everything, shrinking and forming into a beautiful, perfect sphere about five times the size of a beach ball, hovering above the five-pointed star. It looked almost like a miniature planet, flashes of silver and blue swirling around it like clouds. I'd seen it before, when it was first created. FrostNight.

Lord Dogknife shook me again, and I felt something shift in my pocket—*right*! Josephine's switchblade . . .

I relaxed my grip on his hand, slowly going limp like I was losing consciousness, and let my arms fall to my sides. He laughed in my face, and I smelled the awful scent of death again.

I felt my feet touch the floor as he lowered me slightly, though it wasn't enough to find purchase or stand. The tiles slid beneath my heels as he dragged me over to the star, to where FrostNight waited.

Wind rushed against my skin, and I heard the flapping of wings as Jo launched herself at Lord Dogknife. Through barely open eyes, I saw her wielding a long, thin piece of metal like a spear; she must have lost the blaster. Lord Dogknife ducked out of the way as she came at him, and I used his motion to disguise mine as I reached into my pocket for the little knife.

Jo rushed past him as he dodged, expertly wheeling around in the air and kicking off against the wall to come at him again. This time he was ready for her and grabbed the bit of metal out of the air as she thrust it at him.

I drew in as much breath as I could—not easy, considering

the viselike grip he had on my throat—and flipped the knife open, raising my arm to strike as he threw Jo back against the far wall.

The blade bit down into his outstretched arm, cutting deep. He howled, the fingers that had been curled around my neck snapping open reflexively as the weapon sliced through skin and tendons.

My feet touched the floor more firmly for a precious half second before his other arm snapped out, managing to grab the front of my shirt. I felt his claws scrape against the skin of my chest as he scrabbled for whatever hold on me he could get, and my back collided with the tile as he shoved me down.

"Insolent child!" he roared. Dark blood dripped sluggishly from the knife still stuck in his arm. "I'll give you to FrostNight piece by piece!"

"Joey!" Jakon yelled from off to my left, but I was pinned to the ground by Lord Dogknife's strong grip.

He slashed at my face with razor-sharp black claws, and all I could do was turn my head and shut my eyes. The pain went through me so quickly I didn't even comprehend it at first; the adrenaline pumping through my system kept me from feeling it for a few precious seconds longer.

I felt the tile against the right side of my face, the coolness of it sharply contrasted with the burning pain starting to throb on the left side. In a moment of lucidity, I realized I couldn't feel that iron grip on my shirt anymore—I tried to open my eyes, and caught a glimpse of Jakon clinging to Lord Dogknife, slashing at him with her own claws. My vision seemed somehow sideways, and everything was blurry, tinted red. I crawled away from them, numb, some detached part of my brain noting the drops of blood falling from my face to splash crimson against the white floor.

The pain I'd started to feel sharpened into nothing less than agony. I felt sick. Even worse than how much I hurt was the abrupt feeling of *wrongness*, of my skin feeling too big for my face. I couldn't see out of my left eye at all.

"Joe!" Acacia's voice reached my ears over the rush of wind, the blaster shots and various other sounds of fighting. "Get out of here!"

I struggled to my knees and put a hand up to my face, fighting the wave of nausea that came over me. With one eye covered like I was about to take a vision test, I found Acacia's lean figure in the crowd. I couldn't tell how far away she was.

She and Avery had traded places; she was now standing over her wounded brother and using his sword to fend off attacks from Lady Indigo. There were several Walkers down here and there, some of them alone and some being defended by their comrades.

If the Walkers hadn't gotten here, we wouldn't have stood a chance. Avery and Acacia wouldn't have been able to free me by themselves. They had come, risking their lives, to save me. They were buying me time to run.

It wouldn't help. Unless Acacia was able to defeat Lady Indigo where her brother had failed (I didn't even know if "kill" was the right word; for all I knew, it might take more than that), Lord Dogknife would just use her to power Frost-Night. He'd said so himself. It might not be as strong, but it would still continue. More worlds would be destroyed. All this fighting and all this death, and it was all for nothing.

I looked up, finding the perfect sphere sitting calm and beautiful amid the chaos, perhaps twenty steps in front of me. *He comes for you*, Lord Dogknife had said. It struck me suddenly, for the first time, that he hadn't said *it*.

I couldn't stop it. The words from when I'd first woken up in chains came back to me, said in a voice I couldn't quite place. It was my voice, but not.

A sound reached my ears over all the chaos, like the white noise of a radio left on. As I tried to push myself to my feet, gaze locked on the floor beneath me, a pair of brown shoes stepped into my line of sight. I looked up, meeting the Professor's static gaze.

"Running is useless, Walker," he said. "You must know this by now. Why not accept your fate?" His voice was even and human sounding, but completely emotionless, like it was dialogue plugged into a computer. There was a kind of electronic quality to it, too, something that was *too* smooth, too contrived.

I ignored him, still struggling to stand. I felt dizzy and

sick, like the floor was going to slide out from beneath me any moment. I cast around for a portal, didn't sense one— but I did sense Hue, hovering worriedly nearby. Maybe he could make me a portal.

Hue, I thought, but my resolve weakened. He couldn't hear me unless we were merged, or whatever it was he did, and anyway, the Professor was right: Running wasn't the answer. Running wouldn't solve anything.

I finally got to my feet, standing as tall as I could to look at the Professor. He regarded me critically, like a teacher waiting impatiently for an answer.

"The decision is yours, Harker," he said. "Either accept your fate, as those have before you, or attempt to run. You may even make it a few steps before you are caught."

As those have before you. The words reminded me of something else I'd heard him say when I'd been hooked up to the machine that had first powered FrostNight. *You will fulfill your purpose and bring about the revolution of the world*, he'd said, and Joaquim had struggled against his bonds as he realized his fate. *No,* he'd screamed. *I don't want to—*

I remembered his face when I'd tried to help him, his dead eyes. I remembered the words I'd heard upon waking.

Isn't this my destiny?

"Hue," I said, and the little mudluff brightened. If he merged with me again, I'd be able to Walk anywhere. I could probably even find my way to TimeWatch itself, but I had a better idea.

Well, it wasn't technically a *better* idea. In fact, it was probably the worst idea I'd ever had, and that was saying a lot.

I held out my hand to Hue and he came to perch on my palm. He seemed to sense what I wanted through the contact, and began to flow up my arm like liquid. The Professor's eyes narrowed and he raised a hand, but I took a step toward him instead of away, and he paused.

"I know my purpose," I told him. "It's something that's so much a part of me—of all of us—that nothing you do can shake it. Even when you boil us down to our very essence, or freeze us and keep us alive to help you Walk, we still know our purpose."

Hue flowed over my body, over my face and my wounded eye. "Our purpose is to stop you," I said. "And not even death will take that from us."

And with that, I Walked—but not to the In-Between, or even sideways to a parallel world. I Walked exactly twenty steps forward, reappearing in front of the perfect silver and blue sphere. As I looked back, the Professor's static eyes met mine, and the corners of his mouth tilted up in the barest hint of pleasure. I heard Acacia scream my name again, and Joeb. I saw J/O and Jai, lying still by the giant, smoking computer.

Jakon and Josef were taking on Lord Dogknife, and Jo had flown over to help Acacia again. The floor was littered with Binary clones and Walkers alike, and FrostNight waited in front of me, peaceful and hungry and alone.

I turned my back on the chaos, and started forward. Like going off the diving board into the deep end, I took a running start and jumped, plunging headfirst into the heart of FrostNight.

Isn't this my destiny?

CHAPTER TWELVE

Have you come to GLOAT?

As before, the words just seemed to hang in the air, unspoken but somehow still present. I opened my eyes—both of them, and I felt no pain—and looked around, but at first there was nothing to see. There was nothing but soft light, pale and colorless, and what looked like static in the distance.

"Where am I?" I asked. I looked down at my hands and my body.

The eye of the storm.

I recognized the cloth covering my arms, and it wasn't what I'd been wearing when I went in. It was a green and black hoodie—my favorite hoodie, the one I'd been wearing when I Walked for the first time. I'd forgotten it at home—the home that was now gone—when I'd packed up some of my things and left the life I knew forever.

Yet here it was. I could feel the softness of the material, could smell the detergent my parents always used. I was wearing my most comfortable pair of jeans, and the ratty sneakers I'd worn into the ground. I felt no wounds anywhere on my body, which I *knew* was impossible.

I looked around again, trying to find the source of the voice I couldn't hear. If I squinted, I could see that what I'd thought was static was actually lots of tiny numbers and letters. It was like what I'd seen back on my world. It was the swirling storm of FrostNight, and I was at the very center.

It was calm here, and quiet, though there was an underlying uneasiness boiling beneath the surface. A rage, something that felt like what you'd see in a wounded animal. Betrayal. Pain. Confusion.

"Joaquim," I said, my own voice sounding strange to me. I sounded younger, my voice lacking the rough edge of the growth I'd already gone through. "Joaquim, this is you, isn't it?"

That was the name we were given. The words came to me. I felt a faint rush of relief; my gamble had paid off. I'd been right about the "he" Lord Dogknife mentioned. Joaquim's consciousness still existed within FrostNight, which meant I might be able to reason with him. I might be able to convince him to stop this.

Slowly, so slowly I thought I was imagining it at first, I became aware of little sparks of blue light. They winked in and out like stars in a cloudy sky, twinkling and seeming to move. There were more and more of them until they came together, forming a figure I recognized. He looked like me, as so many of us did.

"It is you," I said. "You're alive."

I was never alive, he said, though the little blue stars that made up his mouth didn't move.

I took a breath. Technically, he was right. Joaquim had been a clone, grown by Binary from our blood and powered by the souls of those killed by HEX. But . . . he'd had a personality, a consciousness. He'd had desires and goals, and in the end he'd wanted to live when he'd been told it was his destiny to die.

"Yes, you were. You were your own consciousness, different from the souls used to power you. You knew your identity. You considered HEX and Binary your parents, and you felt betrayed when they used you. You were alive, and you wanted to stay that way."

He formed into something more substantial in front of me, into the person I remembered. His hair was dark, skin pale, eyes brown. I could still see the glimmering lights at certain points on his body, like he was an image superimposed over a field of stars, a constellation given form.

"You still consider yourself a child," he said, and this time his lips moved and the voice that issued forth was the one I remembered.

"What?"

"You exist only as your consciousness here," he explained. "As do I. You have a body because you are used to having one, and thus you give it the form you most identify with."

"You mean, this is how I see myself?" I asked, glancing down. I wished I had a mirror, but I was pretty sure I knew what I'd see: a young, kind of goofy-looking kid who was in way over his head.

It wasn't really surprising to learn that was how I still saw myself. It was pretty accurate.

He nodded. I looked him over, taking him in. His image was faint, like an echo, and I could see the souls used to power him far more clearly than I saw him. I wondered if this was how he saw himself as well.

"That was you I heard, wasn't it? When I woke up?"

He hesitated. "I was not sure if you *had* heard me. Your consciousness brushed mine as you were extracted from your Earth."

"What do you mean, 'extracted'?"

"It was the Professor's wish that you be saved for later use."

I remembered the last few moments on my world, with all the figures swirling around me. Some of them had come toward me, covering me like a swarm of bees, and I'd felt myself fragmenting. I'd been broken down into my most basic chemistry, and re-formed elsewhere. It was basic teleportation, really.

"He wanted FrostNight to absorb me, to use my energy," I said. Joaquim nodded. "Did you stop it?"

"It was not possible right then. The worlds that were destroyed were broken down and restarted clean so my parents can enforce their will upon them. Taking you at that time was not in my protocol."

My mind whirled. He had just told me two very important things, and I wasn't sure which meant more. One filled me with hope that was immediately quashed; the other filled me with anger.

If my world had been *restarted*, that meant, in a sense, it wasn't dead. If the planet was left alone, there was the smallest chance that maybe life would evolve as it had before. There was the smallest, tiniest chance that maybe my family would live again someday. I'd be long dead by the time that happened, but it was something, at least.

The other thing was his saying *my protocol.* This told me something *very* important.

"You're not just within FrostNight," I said. "You *are* Frost-Night. You're its consciousness."

"Yes."

"Then why didn't you stop it?" I screamed at him, the words ripping themselves from me. He didn't even blink.

"Should I have?" he asked. I stared at him, aghast, and he continued. "Why? Why should I have stopped?"

"Because you just killed—" I had to pause, the number

so high I couldn't even fathom it. "Innocent people. Billions upon billions of innocents."

"Yes," he agreed. "That was a side effect of my ultimate purpose."

I continued to just stare at him. Several other thoughts were making their way through my head; if he *was* Frost-Night, if he was its heart, maybe killing him would stop it.

The problem was, I wasn't even sure I *could* kill him. Not just physically, but morally. I felt for him. Even knowing he'd allowed the destruction of an indeterminate number of worlds, including mine, I felt for him. He hadn't asked to be created for this, and he certainly hadn't asked to have his consciousness shoved into a mash-up of science and sorcery made for the sole purpose of eradicating all life.

Still, his unfortunate circumstances didn't entirely excuse his lack of personal responsibility, if you wanted to break it down to simple psychology.

Personal responsibility . . .

"But you said you were sorry," I reminded him. "I heard you, remember? You said you were sorry you couldn't stop it."

His whole body flickered as though he might fade out, as though I'd shaken his very reality. "Yes," he agreed hesitantly.

"If this is your purpose, and what you want to do, why be sorry?"

"It . . . is my purpose," he said. "I did not say it is what I want to do."

"Then change it!"

"I don't know how."

"You're a self-aware ripple in time and space with the power to recalibrate entire worlds! The *how* is easy—stop doing it!"

"I can't exist any other way," he snapped. "This is what I was made for! You're asking me to stop existing!"

The words hung in the silence, ringing true for both of us. I just looked at him, my sympathy growing with sudden certainty. "Yes," I said. "That's exactly what I'm asking you to do."

"Why should I?" he asked bitterly. "Why should I, when I could just take your power now and sustain myself forever?"

"Because what kind of existence would that be?" I asked, struggling to keep a lid on my temper. "Even if you fulfill your purpose and reshape the entire Multiverse for HEX and Binary, then what? Do you really think Lord Dogknife will wave his magic wand and make you into a real boy?"

He wavered again. "I . . ."

"Or that the Professor will grow you another body to live in? You're *made from us*, Joaquim. You're not a machine like Binary, they won't want you. You don't fit into their equation, their dream of a perfect, cold, and calculated existence. You're not an entirely organic being like HEX, and you have no magic except what they gave you. And that magic," I continued, desperate to drive the point home, "comes from *us*. From the things they hate."

He stared at me, his expression saying more than his silence. He looked hurt and vulnerable, like a child. "You're not one of them, Joaquim," I pressed. "Of either of them."

"And what am I, then?" he snapped, the little blue lights of his body pulsing with electric anger. "One of *you*?"

"Yes," I said. "You are."

He went still, surprised and wary. "You don't mean that," he said. "You are just trying to get me to stand down. Negotiation Tactics in High Stress Situations, Lesson One, Reasoning with Your Opponent by Identifying—"

"Joaquim, *listen to yourself*!" I interrupted. "Yes, I am identifying with you, because you're *just like me*. I hate that you were made by my enemies, I hate that you betrayed us—but I hate that they betrayed you, too! You wanted to live, and you should have been given the chance. I wanted to save you," I admitted, surprised by the words as they tumbled from my lips. "I tried to save you, at the end. I'm sorry I couldn't."

He continued to look at me, still wary and suspicious, but I could tell he was remembering. He was remembering all the lights and the fires and the wind, and the machines we'd both been hooked up to, and how he'd held his hand out to me and I'd taken it.

"So if I'm just like you," he said finally, keeping his tone even and betraying nothing, "what would you do? If this was your only chance at existing, what would you do?"

"I'd give it up," I said immediately. "I would stop it."

"You would die."

"Yes."

"You would willingly die?"

"To save everything? Yes."

He stared at me, then finally shuddered and looked away. "I don't believe you," he whispered. "It's easy to say you're willing to die, but to actually do it . . . to simply *not exist* . . . to miss out on *everything* . . ."

"I'll prove it," I said, holding out my hand. "Take me."

He looked up. "What?"

"Take my power. Absorb me."

He looked at my hand like it was a trap, hesitating.

Hue, I thought at the presence in the back of my mind. *This is your chance to get out now, little buddy. Tell the others it's okay, and I'll miss them. Tell them Joeb's in charge.*

There was the general feeling of negation from somewhere inside my head. *Hue, do you understand what I'm about to do?*

Acceptance.

You'll die, bud. I don't want that. Go on.

Negation.

Hue, go on*! You have to tell them for me!*

Negation, sympathy, acceptance.

You're one in a million, buddy.

Agreement. It struck me that Hue, despite being of a race many of us feared, had proven himself time and again to be a valuable teammate. I almost laughed out loud, and I wondered suddenly if Hue might actually be one of us, too. Joseph Harker, multidimensional life-form edition. Hell, it didn't seem that unlikely.

"Absorb my power," I said again to Joaquim, still holding out my hand. "I have Hue with me right now, I can see and understand a lot more than if I were by myself. Let me join with you, with FrostNight, and I'll stop it. I'll destroy it from the inside. You won't have to do a thing."

"I'll still die," he whispered.

"And so will I, and so will Hue. But everyone else will live, and that's more important than anything." He hesitated again, and I took a breath, grasping at straws.

"You have the memories of a hundred different Walkers, Joaquim—you said that once. Right?"

He nodded.

"You have the memories of their deaths, right?"

He hesitated again. "Some of them . . ."

"Can you honestly tell me that none of them went into this knowing and accepting that they might die?"

He flinched. Some of the lights within him grew dimmer, others brighter. "They were so afraid. . . . ," he whispered.

"Of course they were afraid. *I'm* afraid. I don't want to die," I admitted, feeling my stomach tighten into a knot with the truth of it. "But if it's the only way to save everything, I will. You know I will. Come on. You and me,

Joaquim. The saviors of the Multiverse."

He snapped his head up, looking into my eyes, then at my hand. He moved, translucent and shimmering and glowing with the memories of a hundred lives. He took my hand.

"I, Joseph Harker," I said. He looked at me.

"I . . . Joaquim . . ." Here he stopped, and I realized he didn't have a last name.

"Harker," I said. "You're one of us."

"I . . . Joaquim Harker," he whispered, and I took his other hand.

"Understanding that there must be balance in all things . . ."

His voice joined mine, and we said the oath together, as the walls of FrostNight whipped and whirled around us. I could feel it constricting with me inside, felt it closing around the edges of my consciousness. I was afraid, but also calm. Peaceful. I could do this. I could save everyone. I could put Joaquim to rest, and all the souls that were part of him.

I hadn't been able to save my family, but I could save everyone else's.

Mom, Dad, Jenny, Kevin . . . I love you.

I felt my mind becoming one with FrostNight. It was chaotic and perfect, the answer on the edge of everything, the truth just out of reach. It was the precipice of all and nothing.

I felt my body break into pieces, my consciousness ceasing

to need it as a vessel. FrostNight was my vessel now, and it was all I would ever be.

I was aware of everything outside myself, of the battle still raging. I found the threads of time connecting Avery and Acacia, and all the little stars that were my fellow Walkers. I gathered them all up like the strings of a hundred balloons, releasing them into the sky and sending them off toward InterWorld. Toward freedom.

I found the blight that was HEX, the virus that was Binary. They existed in the Multiverse like rot in wood, like decay on death. Necessary, in moderation. I had the power to destroy them. I did not.

I felt Joaquim react within my consciousness, and I felt him understand. I felt him join me as I began the process of deconstructing us, of pulling FrostNight apart piece by piece.

Then, like a ship with its tether cut, I felt a jarring sense of dislocation. I was floating, adrift, and then I knew no more.

CHAPTER THIRTEEN

I UNDERSTAND NOW, JOEY. *You didn't ask any-thing of me you weren't willing to give yourself. You truly would have died for everyone.*

That was enough.

"Joaquim?"

"He's awake," someone said. It was a man's voice, one I didn't recognize.

I fought to open my eyes, but as before, my vision was off. All I could see were vague shapes, blurred and distorted, like looking into a funhouse mirror. My face felt strange, and all the little aches and pains I'd been suffering for the past however long (it felt like forever) were back. They were *really* back. I groaned.

"Hey, you," another voice said, accompanied by a slight dip in whatever surface I was resting on as someone sat down on it. This voice, I recognized.

I turned my head toward her, managing to make out the faint shape of her. I both heard and felt the crinkle of bandages around my face, covering my left eye.

Covering my eye. I remembered Lord Dogknife's claws, the ripping pain and the intense burning, the blood falling to the perfect white floor. Was my eye . . . ? "Acacia," I mumbled. "Where's Joaquim?"

I felt her take my hand. "Joaquim died a long time ago, Joe. Remember? When FrostNight was first—"

"He *is* FrostNight," I insisted. "He's the consciousness of FrostNight. . . ."

Her hand squeezed mine. "Okay," she said, and it sounded like she understood. After a moment, she spoke again. I could barely make out the sadness in her expression as she did. "Then you mean 'was,' Joe. FrostNight is gone."

I took a breath, held it, let it out slowly. More of my vision cleared, enough that I could see her sitting next to me.

She looked like she'd been through hell. Her dark hair was tied back into a ponytail, and she was wearing an oversized sweatshirt that was so thin and worn it had to have belonged to someone else first. The faded words said *Alpha-Cen Med School.* It looked comfortable. The sleeves were rolled up, revealing some of her injuries.

There were a dozen little cuts and bruises up and down both arms, half-healed ones from when she'd come crashing onto InterWorld and new ones from her fight with Lord

Dogknife and Lady Indigo. Her eyes were red, like she'd been crying.

My face itched. I reached up with my free hand to rub at it, watching her expression go from relieved to concerned as she watched me. "You shouldn't touch it for a while," she said. "While it heals."

My fingers encountered the soft gauze and bandages, and she offered me a faint smile, hand tightening around mine.

"*Will* it heal?" I asked. I was pretty sure I already knew the answer.

"We did what we could, but the HEX hound's claws were vicious," the unfamiliar voice from before said, and I looked up to see a tall man with dark hair and a neatly trimmed goatee standing by my bed.

"Dad's the best healer we've got," Acacia said earnestly. "He really did the best he could, Joe."

Dad?

I blinked up at the tall man, who was looking at his daughter with sympathy. There might have been a resemblance, but it was hard to tell with the facial hair. "I'm sure he did," I mumbled reassuringly to Acacia. They'd done all they could. Did that mean they hadn't been able to fix it? Had I lost my eye?

That would be ironic. The thought came unbidden to my mind, and I bit down on the inside of my cheek to keep from laughing. It seemed to be a nervous habit of mine, and one I should probably try to break.

"What happened?" I asked instead.

"We were all fighting," Acacia said slowly. "And then you . . . ran into FrostNight." She glared at me. "Which was *stupid*, and reckless . . ."

"Just tell me what happened."

She glared for another moment, then continued. "I felt you gather us all up, but . . . I also felt FrostNight constrict. It fell in on itself, and I went back to find you. You were lying there, in the middle of the star."

"He saved me," I murmured. She just looked at me. "We were going to destroy FrostNight together. He must have pushed me out at the last minute."

She hesitated, then squeezed my hand again. "That makes sense."

I actually did laugh this time, but bitterly. "How does any of this make sense?"

Acacia glanced up at her father, then looked back to me. "Well . . . Binary are, of course, machines. They don't understand things like souls and free will, so they wouldn't have thought that Joaquim could do anything other than fulfill his directive. HEX *does* understand how souls work, but they believe themselves to have ultimate power over them . . . so they, also, could not have predicted Joaquim's capacity for free will. You're the one who showed him that, Joe. You showed him he had a choice, and by choosing to die"—her gaze got a bit more intense; I think she didn't entirely approve of that decision—"you showed him that he, also, had a choice. And he chose to save you."

I was surprised at how little I felt. I supposed I was probably in shock. I had expected to die, and in the end, Joaquim had saved me like I hadn't been able to save him. I remained silent, thinking, remembering those last moments. Finally, I found another question.

"Where's Hue?"

"Well," Acacia's father said, "that's the other thing. The MDLF seems to have taken up permanent residence inside your body, and we have been unable to extract him."

"Extract . . . ?"

"When you were expelled from FrostNight, you were one. It seems you still are, and I am not certain it can be undone. Beyond that, I believe he is helping to heal your eye."

I frowned, then immediately winced as the expression pulled at the skin around my eyes. Hue was bound with me? And was helping to heal my eye? He'd never shown any kind of healing ability before. And he'd taken up permanent residence inside my body?

Hue? I thought, but got no response. I was aware of him now that I concentrated, dimly, but . . .

To distract myself, I looked around.

I was obviously in an infirmary, but an unfamiliar one. There were some machines I recognized and others I didn't at all, and the overall color scheme was odd for an infirmary. Instead of the stark white I was used to, there were mahogany wood cabinets, pinkish marble floors, beige walls. Despite my not recognizing the room, something about it was naggingly familiar.

"Where am I?" I asked.

"TimeWatch," Acacia said. "Sick bay."

That would explain the familiar colors. I'd been to Time-Watch once before, when Acacia had taken me captive. . . .

"I'm not a prisoner, am I?"

She at least had the grace to look vaguely embarrassed at the reminder. "No," she said pointedly, setting her shoulders and lifting her chin. "And you weren't a prisoner before, I was just trying to—"

"I'm teasing you," I interrupted. "Settle down. Where is everyone else?" I asked, suddenly worried for my friends. I remembered sending them all off to InterWorld, but . . . "Are they okay?"

"They're here," she reassured me, nodding. "They're all down at the docks. We're getting your ship fixed up," she added with a smile.

"My ship . . . ?"

"InterWorld," she clarified. "Duh."

"You really just said *duh*."

"Yeah, I did. I'm a Time Agent, I can use whatever slang I want."

"I'm glad to see you feeling better, young man," her father interrupted, and we both quieted. "But I do have other patients to attend to. You are free to go, with an escort, and the bracelet on your wrist can be used to call for medical aid if you need it."

"Thanks, Daddy," Acacia said, and he smoothed her hair back affectionately as he went by. My heart ached.

"Thank you," I managed. I waited until he was gone, then lowered my voice. "Is that really your father?"

"Yes," she said, smiling. "And my mother is currently on deck, and Avery is really my brother." I was going to ask her what "on deck" meant, but her smile faded and she glanced off toward another of the hospital beds. I followed her gaze, noting the sheathed sword leaning up against the wall near the headboard. I couldn't see who occupied the bed, but by the sword, I assumed it to be Avery.

"Is he okay?" I asked. She bit her lip, forehead wrinkling as her eyes watered.

"Probably," she said, her voice tight. "Dad's taking really good care of him. I'm just . . . we lose people all the time."

"I know how that is," I said.

"I know you do." She took my hand again.

"Is he your only sibling?" I asked after a moment. I was genuinely curious; I had wondered, once, if TimeWatch was an organization made up of Acacias like InterWorld was made up of Joeys, but that didn't seem to be the case.

"No," she said, looking a little happier. "I have an older sister and a younger one. And a ton of aunts and uncles and cousins."

"So, TimeWatch is basically . . . just your whole family?"

"It's a few different families. Mine, and a couple of others. They aren't *exactly* my cousins. . . . It's hard to explain. Suffice to say you aren't the only one with other versions of you running around."

"Oh, no," I said. When she looked at me quizzically, I squinched my face carefully into an expression of distaste. "There's more than one of you?"

"You're a jerk," she told me.

"Am not," I said. "I've just had a bad . . . everything." The truth of it hit me and I looked away, recalling how much I'd been through and how much I still had to grieve for. "Acacia . . . when you found your way back to InterWorld and Avery said you were out of sync with our timestream, or whatever . . . When you told me my world was in FrostNight's path . . ." I started. She hung her head. "You said you'd try to help," I continued, tilting my head to try to look into her eyes. "You said TimeWatch would help, and you didn't—"

"We did," she said sharply, lifting her head again. "My aunt died there. She did everything she could."

I felt a little better knowing they'd tried, and also felt bad that she'd lost someone there, too—was that what I'd seen in all the chaos, when I thought there had been a woman there with the Old Man?—but I was still upset that whatever they'd done hadn't helped. "It was still destroyed. I'm sorry you lost your aunt, but what did she *do*, exactly?"

"She reversed it," Acacia snapped, trying to pull her hand from mine. I let her, keeping my expression calm, to reassure her I just wanted answers. "She couldn't actually stop Frost-Night from wiping the world clean, but she created a custom timestream for it. It'll run parallel to the anchor, now."

"What does that mean?"

"It means it was restarted rather than destroyed, and it'll progress faster than others of its timestream would as compared to a fixed point."

"The anchor."

"Yes."

"And what's the anchor?"

"You," she said, meeting my gaze.

I took a moment to let that sink in. "Me?"

"Yes."

"So . . . my planet was restarted."

"Yes. And things should progress on it, barring outside interference—which we will work to ensure—exactly as they did previously."

I sat there in silence, digesting this. My world was *not* dead, but technically, my family still was. Technically, *everything* was . . . but it wouldn't always be. Things would live again. My family would live again, someday.

It wasn't much comfort, really, but it was something.

"I'm sorry about your aunt," I said.

"Thank you," she said softly. "I'll miss her. I wish you could have met her. She knew Captain Harker."

"Really," I asked, but it wasn't a question.

"Mhm," she said. I felt like a couple of different mysteries were on the verge of being solved here, but I was too tired to examine them closely. All I knew was that I was here, and relatively safe, and InterWorld was here, too. Joaquim had come through in the end, saving me and sacrificing himself. HEX and Binary were crippled for a while, at least, and we were getting a boost in technology from TimeWatch.

None of that made up for how many lives had been lost. But then, nothing ever would.

"Mom wanted to talk to you when you were up for it," Acacia said.

"I'm up for it," I told her. Honestly, I had some questions of my own.

"Are you sure?"

"Yeah. I feel like I've been in bed for days."

"Two days," she said. "To be exact."

I pushed the covers back, moving my legs carefully over the side of the bed. I was wearing clothing I didn't recognize, but it was comfortable and clean, which was a big plus. "Yeah, I'm definitely ready to get up."

"I don't know if you should yet, Joe."

"Your father said I'm free to move around," I said.

"With an escort," she reminded me, giving another smile. "I guess it's my turn to play tour guide, huh?"

"Sure is," I said. "Just warn me in advance if you're going to do any abrupt time-warping, okay?"

"I'll do my best," she said, helping me stand. "Where to?" she asked, once I'd found my balance.

"The docks," I said. "I want to see my ship."

The docks of TimeWatch were a lot like I'd have expected; half a dozen long wooden walkways extending off into the distance, with various types of ships from all different cultures and time periods docked at them. It was odd to see InterWorld (which was big enough to house more than five hundred people) tied to someone else's dock like some little dinghy. It was huge, easily one of the largest ships there, and it was still dwarfed by the sheer scale of TimeWatch.

Acacia and I stood on a platform overlooking everything. Beneath the docks was an ocean of something other than water; it looked more like a nebula, with swirls of deep blue and green and white, and sparkles of little stars like sea foam. The sky was that beautiful amalgamation of colors and galaxies I'd seen when I'd first been to TimeWatch.

It was like there were a million skies all mashed up into one, the sun rising and setting multiple times in minutes, in a hundred different places. There were moons and stars and clouds and fog, all sharing the same sky. It had been beautiful before, when I'd been a prisoner uncertain of my fate. Now, standing here overlooking it as a guest assured of his safety, it was breathtaking.

My ship was all lit up, warm and inviting like lights seen through the windows of a familiar house. She sat amid the waves of stars, making little ripples as people moved off and on, carrying supplies and machinery. Some of those people were obviously my friends, the Walkers who'd made it out of the fight unscathed, and others must have been the other TimeWatch families Acacia had mentioned. It was refreshing to see so many people who weren't me.

Acacia and I stood there for a while, watching everyone move about below us. I still felt incomplete, somehow, like things hadn't been entirely resolved. Like it was all so unfinished. I didn't feel accomplished, like I had actually saved anyone. In the end, Joaquim had been the one to make the sacrifice that saved us, and I couldn't give him the recognition he deserved for it.

"There's Mom," Acacia said finally, pointing. "And that's my little sister with her."

I looked where she indicated, picking out a dark-haired woman in a long coat standing with a clipboard in her hand. A younger girl stood next to her, something in her hands occasionally flashing white and lighting up her surroundings.

"Lead the way," I said, though she wound up having to physically lead me, as trying to navigate the long stairway with only one working eye proved a lot more difficult than I'd thought. My depth perception was way off, and I took a few of the steps harder than I meant to by misjudging the distance. By the time we got to the bottom, my ribs were aching again from the jarring missteps.

"Mom," Acacia called, and the woman turned. As expected, she looked a lot like an older Acacia; they had the same jaw, same nose, same violet eyes. Her hair was lighter, though, and her face was subtly different. Not her smile, though. Her smile was the same.

"Joseph Harker," she said, tucking her clipboard under one arm and offering me her hand. I took it. Instead of shaking, she covered it with her other hand, the gesture surprisingly warm. I thought of my own mother, and swallowed.

"Hi," I said, glancing down at the little girl peering around from behind her mother. She, also, bore a slight resemblance to Acacia.

"I'm Deana," Acacia's mother said, releasing my hand. "It's a pleasure to finally meet you."

"You, too," I said awkwardly, stumbling over the niceties, but she didn't seem to notice. She was already turning toward InterWorld and looking down at her clipboard again. I caught a glimpse of what looked like blueprints and a lot of technical words even I didn't recognize.

"She's almost ready for you, Captain Harker," Deana said, and I tried not to cringe.

"I—I'm not—"

"Don't even try," she interrupted. "With the death of Captain Joseph Harker Omega, you most certainly are the new captain of InterWorld."

"Joseph . . . Omega?" I asked. She shrugged.

"We have our own classifications to keep everything straight." Before I could respond to that, she started walking. She kept talking, too, obviously expecting me to follow. I did.

"We're making some upgrades," she continued, pointing a long silver pen toward InterWorld. "Mainly in your security system, since there was obviously a breach. Two, at least, which is why—"

"Mrs. Jones," I interrupted. "Can you tell me—"

"Call me Deana."

"What happened to this InterWorld? Why it was abandoned?"

She stopped walking again, regarding me with kind amusement. Then she glanced past me, at Acacia. "All the questions he could ask, and he asks about something that doesn't concern him."

Acacia smiled and shrugged. "It concerns InterWorld, which means it concerns him."

"That event occurs tens of thousands of years in the

future, Joseph," Deana said.

"Time isn't static," I said, repeating something I remembered Acacia saying. "That event may have already occurred in the future, but that doesn't mean it won't affect me."

Her expression changed. She looked at me for a long, uncomfortable moment, and I recalled something Jay had said a long time ago about how it was TimeWatch's job to make sure the future happens as it's supposed to, and how they could erase me if it became necessary. . . .

Then she looked at Acacia again, who cleared her throat uncomfortably. "Mom, uh . . ."

"You're grounded," her mother said, and the girl behind her giggled. Acacia's eyes widened, mouth dropping open in faint outrage.

"You're kidding me," Acacia said, and Deana laughed.

"Yes, I am kidding. Your brother already told me how much Joseph knows about time, in part due to the MDLF," Deana explained, looking down at her clipboard again. "To that end, the council has decided to appoint an official liaison on his missions." She glanced at me. "No offense, but someone has to make sure he doesn't inadvertently mess up the timestreams."

I shrugged. Acacia blinked.

"A liaison?"

"Yes," her mother said. "Go pack."

I looked at Acacia. She looked at me and abruptly broke

into a wide grin. "That means I get to tell you what to do," she said.

"No, it means you get to tell me what *not* to do, and it doesn't mean I'll listen," I said. I was mostly teasing her back, but something about this arrangement still rubbed me the wrong way. "Assuming I even accept this deal."

Deana gave me an amused look. "Assuming you accept?"

"You just said this is my ship. Like it or not, that means I'm in charge of InterWorld and everyone in it, *and* continuing the fight against Binary and HEX. I have enough on my plate without having to worry about TimeWatch telling me what I can or can't do. If you're so bent on controlling us, why don't you take over the fight?"

"We have our own problems," Acacia began heatedly, but Deana put a hand on her shoulder.

"I understand how you feel, Joseph. And Acacia is right. The fact is, our problems just became your problems."

"What do you mean?" I asked. Acacia was also looking at her mother curiously.

"I assume my husband told you of the anomaly that bound you to the MDLF?" she asked. I hesitated, but nodded. I still wasn't entirely clear on *how* it happened, but at least I knew what she was talking about. "This same anomaly occurred with the Techs and the Mages, what you know as Binary and HEX. Not with all of them, but with enough. There are a few now who share the characteristics of both, and these are more dangerous than anything you have ever faced—with the exception, I suppose, of FrostNight itself."

Acacia's eyes widened again. "You mean the . . . ?"

"Techmaturges," I said, feeling my stomach descend about to my knees.

"Or something like them," Deana corrected. "They are not exactly the creatures we have faced, but they share some similar abilities. Acacia will be able to help you against them."

I looked at Acacia. She looked slightly less sure about this whole idea now. Her mother reached out to tuck some of her hair back, where it had come loose from her ponytail. "You've studied the most about this timestream, sweetie," she said. "And your brother will take a while to recover. You're the best choice for this mission—everyone thinks so. And you're a Time Agent, Casey. You can come see us whenever you want to."

Acacia visibly cringed at the use of the nickname, scrunching up her face. I couldn't help it; I laughed at her, and she turned a furious glare on me. "I'll slap you again," she warned, and I smiled, remembering how she'd hugged me after.

"Would I get a hug again, if I let you?"

"No." She glared, but then she stepped forward and hugged me anyway. I wasn't entirely sure why, but I knew I was glad to have her in my arms—I was honestly afraid her coming on this mission with me would ruin any chance we had of an actual friendship. Frankly, I hoped hugging her now would help calm me in the future, when I'd inevitably have moments of wanting to strangle her. By the way she sighed, she was likely thinking the same thing.

There was a sudden flash of bright light, and Acacia pulled abruptly back. "Paisley!" she exclaimed, and her sister giggled again. I glanced down at the girl; she was holding what seemed to be an old-fashioned Polaroid camera, which explained the bright lights I'd seen before. She'd been taking pictures of everyone fixing up InterWorld.

Paisley stepped shyly up to me, offering the developing picture. It was white, the chemicals still oxidizing on the film. "Casey hates pictures," she said as I took it from her.

"I also hate that nickname!" Acacia said, reaching for her sister. Paisley ducked and ran off, Acacia not far behind. Deana turned to watch them go, smiling, and then gestured to the photograph.

"You should keep that," she said. I tucked it carefully into my pocket, still looking at her.

"Did you know the Old Man?" I asked. I had a feeling I knew what the answer would be.

"Yes," she said. "We all did, but my sister knew him best."

"Acacia said her aunt died on my world," I said. Deana nodded. "I'm sorry."

"Don't be," she said. "Acacia—my sister, my daughter's

namesake—wasn't sorry. She waited all that time to be able to see him again."

"What do you mean?" I asked. "Why couldn't they see each other?"

"I hope you never find out," she said, handing me the clipboard. "Go on inside," she said, before I could ask again. "I have a few other things to look into, and you have to start restructuring your teams. InterWorld will be ready to go by the end of the day."

She turned and walked away, leaving me with a clipboard I didn't understand and a head full of questions and worries. TimeWatch was like that. I remembered the last part of the Old Man's message, the one he'd had Jaroux record for me. *It's worth it,* he'd said. I wondered if he'd still say so, now.

I moved hesitantly toward InterWorld, unsure of what else to do. My feet did most of the work for me, taking me up the ramp and through the halls without the conscious direction of my mind. I still felt incomplete, like something was missing. I supposed I'd always feel that way. No one had ever said this job was going to be easy.

I walked through the halls, returning the nods and greetings from my fellow Walkers, the infrequent handshakes and even less frequent hugs. No one questioned where I was going; the Old Man's office was mine now, like it or not, and I had work to do. The former members of my team would be officers; they could each take command of their own teams, although I might want to keep Jai as a senior field officer rather than a team leader. Either that, or only assign him Walkers like J/O (and the thought of him immediately brought on another pang of sadness), who had dictionary chips installed in their brains. There had to be others like him out there.

The Old Man's office was just as I'd set it up before leaving to deal with FrostNight, though cleaner. Two of the long silver boxes that now contained all the memories from the Wall were used to hold up the massive slab of marble that served a desk. The others lined the walls, some with padding and cushions to be used as a couch, others used as the base for bookshelves. Morbid as it was, it suited. These memories and the responsibilities that came with them would be mine alone.

I stared at the chair sitting behind the massive desk. I crossed around to stand near it, facing the door. I imagined how this must have looked from the Old Man's point of view, when Walkers came in to debrief after a mission. I wondered if I would ever live that long and get that old. I wondered if young Walkers would fear and respect me the way we had him.

I touched a finger to the surface, watching Josetta's message appear. It was dimmer than it had been; I probably had about a week before it would vanish entirely. I supposed that was for the best, really. It would be a little distracting if it appeared every time I touched my desk.

I slid open a drawer from the standing file cabinet, staring at the stacks of neat office supplies. The contents of the drawer were different from the last time I'd stood here and looked into it, but of course they were; this desk had belonged to someone else. Just like it now belonged to me.

I reached into my pocket, pulling out the picture Acacia's sister had taken of us. It was an actual image now, clear and sharp, Acacia standing with her arms around me and her head resting on my shoulder. She looked sad and hopeful.

As for me, I was a man I didn't recognize. I was tall and strong, my wavy red hair long enough to not look as silly as usual. There were white bandages circling my head and covering one eye, and I looked completely comfortable with the girl in my arms. More than that, I looked determined. I looked wise, like my father—and hard, like the Old Man.

I pulled a pen from the drawer, clicking it open and flipping the picture over. Feeling a little silly, I scribbled on the white part of the Polaroid and stuck it in the back of the drawer.

I left the office, taking Deana's clipboard with me. I wasn't ready to sit there yet, wasn't ready to outline the teams that would be going out and risking their lives to find more of us. I would have to be, later, but for now I would walk the ship. The clipboard detailed more things that needed to be done, and a few of them were things I could do on my own; it suggested an overhaul of the voice recognition and command system, for one.

I walked back through the halls the way I'd come, heading toward the infirmary. The ship was powered up, and I was sure there'd be a few of my friends recuperating here rather than in TimeWatch's sick bay. I was afraid to find out how many of us weren't there, how many hadn't survived the final fight. It was bound to be at least a few, but it always was. It was part of what we signed up for when we came in.

The walls leading up to the infirmary were stark silver, still empty and echoing. I ran my hand absently along them as I walked, feeling the smooth metal pass beneath my hand. This was where the memories of the fallen had been, before I'd taken them down. I'd wanted to give the new recruits a fresh start, to not weigh them down with the memories of those who'd lived and died long after us, still fighting the same war.

This would be a new war, now. The game had changed. Before, I was fighting HEX and Binary to keep my world safe; I was fighting because all the other versions of me were, too, and I could do no less than them. Now I would be leading them, and recruiting more—taking them from their families and giving them the option to fight for their worlds. I wasn't the hero who had saved everyone; I was the cautionary tale, the man who had watched his world die. It was my job now to guide the others in fighting for theirs.

My hand went unbidden up to the chain around my neck, to the pendant I always wore. My mother had made it for me before I'd left home; it was all I had of her now.

I reached up to the clasp behind my neck, unclipping it. I held up the necklace and admired the way the stone caught the light, the black fading to blue and green. It reminded me of the galaxy ocean we floated on, the green of the grass in the park and the blue of the Silver Dream. Of FrostNight. Of Joaquim.

The wall near the infirmary door was patterned with holes from whatever battle had taken place here far in the future, the metal rippled and bent from blaster shots. In one place, it was broken outward enough to form a small hook. I reached up, wrapping the chain around the small bit of metal.

I remembered the Old Man in his last moments, standing there under the tree house. I remembered how peaceful he had looked, and what Acacia had said about my world being restarted. I understood now why he'd been smiling. The world I'd known had died, as everything did eventually—as I had been ready to do, if it meant saving the Multiverse. But it had also lived again, as I had. As my family eventually would.

I had started this to keep my world safe. The war might have changed, but that hadn't.

"Hey, Joe," Acacia's voice came over the com system.

"They restarted all the command systems, and the only voice the software's recognizing is mine. You'd better get up here before I pull a one-woman mutiny and take over the ship!"

I sighed, reaching up to touch the smooth stone of the necklace. "You'd've liked her, Mom," I said. "Though I'm still not sure if I do." A warm feeling flooded through me at that; I could easily imagine my mother's knowing smile as the lie left my lips.

The engines rumbled to life beneath me as I turned to make my way up to the engine room. Even now, my world was growing, forming oceans and trees and clouds. Where it had been like a parent to me, now I saw it as a child. I could still take care of it, still ensure it a long life. I could still protect it. And maybe, if I lived long enough, I could see my family again.

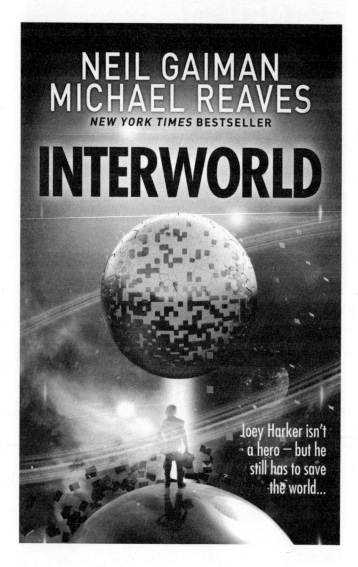